I0732146

LUANN K. EDWARDS

Let Him Go

Love Comes Again Book 2

LuAnn K. Edwards

Dedication

This book is dedicated to my husband Kenn.
Your love and encouragement continue to bless me.

And to my Bible study ladies.
Thank you for being you.

A story of love, acceptance, and forgiveness.

*Jesus looked at them and said, "With man this is impossible,
but with God all things are possible."*
Matthew 19:26

One

Mid-November
Nashville, Tennessee

Blake Conner stood inside our office suite and near my desk when I arrived on Monday morning—our first day back in the office after a business trip together. A lovely mixed bouquet in a clear glass vase sat on my desk.

"They're beautiful." I bent to smell them, straightened, and whispered. "Should you have sent these to me here? I thought we were going to keep our new *friendship* quiet?"

He frowned. "They're not from me. They were on your desk when I arrived." He sounded frustrated. "I'd give you roses." He crossed his arms. "Maybe they're from Wes. I've expected as much."

I stepped over to our office suite door and closed it. "Wes is not your concern. I worked with him in the IT Department, and now we eat lunch together on occasion. That's all." Blake accused me of spending too much time with Wes in the past. I resented him bringing the topic up yet again. I shook my head. "Leave him out of this. They're not from him."

Blake's eyes narrowed. "How many other admirers do you have?"

I responded in an irritated tone. "Perhaps I should open the card to find out."

I grabbed the note from its holder and read to myself. "Keedryn, would you agree to double with Jenny and her husband?" At the bottom, the man included his cell number.

Careful not to react in front of Blake, I showed no emotion and said, "They're from a man my daughter knows from her church."

Blake took a step closer, his tone filled with displeasure. "You dating him?"

"I only met him once—at Jenny's on my birthday a couple of months ago." I pressed my lips together and tried not to smile. But looking at Blake and seeing him watching and waiting for my reaction was rather humorous. "I need to run downstairs and talk to Tauni about your presentation."

I reviewed Blake's PowerPoint slides before we left on our business trip to Albuquerque. He wanted another pair of eyes and called upon Tauni Fisher—an administrative assistant. But when Blake presented at the healthcare conference, he found his slides had been tampered with.

His mouth twitched. "What does the card say?"

I tapped my foot and crossed my arms. "Nothing important."

"Right. Not with that smirk on your face."

"He asked me out." I handed the card to Blake. "Here. Take it."

"Are you going on a date with him?" He flipped the card from front to back.

I sighed. "I'm not interested." I walked behind my desk and placed my purse in my bottom drawer. I hurried past Blake, still staring at the card, and zipped out into the hallway.

Tauni greeted me with a smile. I stood inside her dull, gray cubicle and scanned the photos tacked on her wall. One was of her with her new boyfriend. She said the others were family members.

She asked me about the conference and congratulated me on my new promotion. I would soon become Boden Combs Healthcare's new Admin Services Manager.

Tauni stood and hugged me. "I've applied for your current executive assistant position." She pulled her long, blonde curls behind her ears. "I hope I have a chance."

"I need to ask you something." I lowered my voice. "The slides you reviewed for Blake the day before we left—did anyone else have access to them?"

"I don't remember anything like that." She peered toward the door that led to the hallway. "Wait. Wes stopped by to chat on his way out that afternoon, and he asked whose PowerPoint I was reviewing."

"Wes? Did he ask anything else concerning it?"

"After I told him the presentation was for Blake, he said 'goodbye' and left."

"Did you ever leave your desk while the PowerPoint was open?"

She fiddled with her necklace. "Yes, when Miranda Franks came by."

"Why did someone from HR stop by?"

"She wanted to know which department managers planned to attend the holiday party this year." Tauni shifted her weight to the opposite leg. "She asked me to check right then and there."

"Odd she didn't walk back and ask your manager herself," I said.

"I thought that too."

"How long were you gone?"

"Maybe a couple of minutes." She tilted her head. "Why? What happened?"

"Blake's presentation didn't run smoothly."

"Does he think I did something to it?" Tauni twisted a strand of her hair around her finger. "I didn't change anything. Everything looked perfect to me."

"I assured Blake you wouldn't sabotage him or his presentation."

We discussed how long it took her to read through the slides and what time she completed her review.

Tauni slumped into her chair. "Will this ruin my chance for the executive assistant position?"

"No," I said, smiling. "I think you're good."

"Do you suppose Wes was jealous of you going with Blake to New Mexico?"

Oh, not the accusations about Wes again. In a firm tone, I said, "Wes and I are just friends."

"Couldn't be Miranda. What would she gain?" Tauni picked up a piece of paper from her desk, tore it in half, and tossed it into the trash. "Blake will think I messed up."

I touched her shoulder. "Blake and I will figure everything out. I've got to run. I'll see you later, and don't worry about this."

~

I returned to our office suite. Blake sat at his desk and typed away on his keyboard. "Can we discuss Tauni now?"

He motioned for me to come inside and take a seat at his round, mahogany conference table. He sat next to me and placed the card from my flowers on the table in front of me. "I called that guy for you and told him that you weren't interested."

I stiffened and stared at Blake. "You did what?"

He chuckled. "I wouldn't do that to you." He glanced over at his office door and leaned closer. "Will you join me for dinner tonight?"

I shook my head. "I don't think that's wise. We just spent four days together, and I'm more comfortable with the slower approach."

Blake and I agreed to proceed with caution at the office and keep our friendship between us. He told me that he didn't want me to feel pressured if I wasn't ready for a relationship, and we could move as slowly or as quickly as I felt comfortable. Although he preferred the latter, I was opting for a snail's pace.

"Besides," I said, "you're still planning to come to my house, Thursday, for Thanksgiving dinner, right?"

"I wouldn't miss it." He leaned back and nodded. "I look forward to meeting your family."

"Back to Tauni. Two people stopped by her desk while she worked on your PowerPoint." I picked up the flower card and placed it in my pocket. "Wes—"

Blake sat upright. "That's it. He didn't like you going off with me to New Mexico. Jealousy will cause a man to crack and sabotage a PowerPoint over the woman he loves."

I wilted in my chair. "That's the best you can do?"

"He's IT. He could've easily found the file and destroyed it." He tapped his finger on the table. "Who was the other person?"

"Miranda."

His eyes widened.

I told him that she'd asked Tauni a question that took her away from her desk, which would have given Miranda enough time to find the path on the server for the presentation.

"Why would Miranda mess with my program?"

"You said it yourself. Jealousy?"

"I still think it was Wes."

I placed my hand on my chest and jumped up. *Oh, no.* "I've got to go."

"Where?"

I bolted out of his office, hollering over my shoulder. "I'll be back."

I raced across the hall and stopped in front of Beth Davis's desk where she sat working at her computer. She was the assistant to our president, Chad Warren, my best friend at work, and my prayer partner during struggles with Blake. Before I left for the conference, I'd asked Miranda to offer the promotion to Beth first. I valued our friendship more than an increase in responsibilities and salary.

"How are you today?" I asked.

"Fine." She stared at her monitor.

"Did everything go okay last week?"

"Why wouldn't things be good?" she said in a snooty tone. "Do you think everything falls apart when you're not here?"

"Miranda didn't talk to you, did she?"

Beth glared at me. "Concerning what exactly? Was

she supposed to tell me you were getting another promotion? You and Blake must be getting along well for him to get this position for you."

My mouth fell open.

"Was climbing the corporate ladder your main goal when you came to work here? Or Blake? Playing like he was annoying and arrogant when all the time you two were hitting it off extremely well."

I wrinkled my forehead. "You know how tough this has been for me."

She stood and walked to the front of her desk. "I know nothing except the lies you've been telling me these past several months."

"I don't understand what's happened." I glanced around her office suite. "Miranda said she'd offer the job to you, but if you refused, she'd give the position to me."

"You expect me to believe that?" She clenched her jaw and took a step closer to me. "You've done everything you could to climb over me and everyone else to get what you want."

"Call Blake and ask him what happened."

"Why should I believe him?"

"Call him and ask him to come over here now" I picked up her phone. "I won't have a chance to prep him." I put the receiver back in the cradle. "Or let's go to his office and ask him there. I won't go inside."

I'd never seen Beth this upset. The situation I tried to prevent happened anyway. I hung my head, my thoughts bouncing between getting back at Miranda and proving to Beth she was wrong. I picked up the handset from her desk phone and called Blake myself. I asked if he was available. He said he'd be right over.

"Why are you using my phone?" Beth pulled on the cord. "If I wanted to talk to Blake, I would've called him."

Blake showed up in less than a minute, smiling. "Ladies?"

I turned to face him. "Miranda never talked to Beth."

Beth placed her fists on her hips. "Miranda talks to me all the time."

I clenched my teeth and faced her. "She didn't talk to you regarding the promotion." I pursed my lips and shook my head. "I'm going back to my desk." I looked at Blake and spoke in a frustrated tone. "Please tell her about our conversation last week." I left the two of them to talk privately.

I would not allow Miranda to set me up for failure or interfere with my life. I wrote a short email to her. "I've decided not to accept the offer as Admin Services Manager." I copied Blake and hit send before anyone tried to change my mind.

When Blake returned to our office area, he told me Beth was in our main conference room waiting on me. "She's upset, but after I confirmed you wanted Miranda to offer the job to Beth first, she felt better. Chad came out and got involved too. He assured her that he would investigate the matter." Blake rubbed his chin. "I saw your email pop up on my phone. I support you 100-percent."

I nodded and stood.

Blake walked toward his office, stopped midway, and pivoted toward me. "I checked to see when my presentation was last saved on the server—Wednesday at 4:37 p.m."

"And you loaded the PowerPoint on a flash drive after that?"

"Yes. Around 6:00. A few minutes before I left."

"I'll be right back." I hurried into the conference room.

Beth wiped her eyes when I entered. "I should've known better and believed you. I've brooded over this since the article about your promotion posted on Thursday." She frowned. "I wish you'd told me before you left."

"I should have. Things got busy. And I was sure Miranda talked to you because she told Blake she would." I plopped into the chair next to Beth and exhaled. "When she offered me the position officially, I assumed you knew and weren't interested." I drew my eyebrows together and smoothed out a wrinkled in my skirt.

"A good promotion. I know you'll do a great job. I don't think I would've accepted it." Her shoulders drooped. "But it would have been nice to know there was a position available." Beth folded her hands on the table and stared at them.

"I'd asked Miranda to post the job internally, but she said there wasn't enough time. If I wasn't interested, she said she'd post the position externally." I reached over and touched Beth's hands. "I guess that's what she'll do now."

Her head shot up and she peered at me. "What do you mean? You're not accepting the job?"

"I sent her an email a few minutes ago and told her that I changed my mind."

"I didn't want you to do that. I hope you won't resent me for this later." Tears formed in her eyes again.

"Not at all. Before I came into the office today, I sensed the Lord cautioning me about the position." I shrugged. "Something doesn't feel right."

~

I returned to my office and zipped in to see Blake. "I think all is well with Beth." I sat in the chair in front of his desk.

I related Tauni's information and how she'd completed her review and sent it back to him at 3:50. "Someone else saved it at 4:37. If Miranda, she had plenty of time for sabotage."

Blake cleared his throat. "I know you and Wes are friends, but I still think we should consider him. He could easily find the slides on the server."

"He doesn't seem as likely to me, but I suppose he's a suspect too."

He raised a brow. "Suspect? How are your detective skills?"

I beamed. "I found Andy."

Blake's son, Andy, disappeared five years earlier after his mother's death. He blamed his dad for her accident. While in Albuquerque, we found Andy. I helped in reuniting the two men. Before we flew back to Nashville, Blake met with his son and explained the events that led to his mother's death. Andy realized he'd been wrong about his dad. I was still in the dark regarding the circumstances because Blake's daughter needed to be told before he shared the story with me.

Blake's eyes sparkled. "Maybe you should take the promotion and move downstairs. That might be better for us."

I looked at him with wide eyes. "Us?" He talked

like we were already a couple. "We've just started our *friendship*. Nothing else. Right?"

He leaned back in his chair and ran his hand through his hair. "Whatever you say."

I leaned toward him. "I don't want the position. I need to uncomplicate my life, not make it more challenging. If I take this promotion, Miranda becomes my boss."

"Consider accepting it. Chad's suggestion." He winked.

"Chad? So Beth won't apply?"

"I think it has more to do with what he perceives as our new *friendship*."

"And what does Chad know about that?" I grinned.

He blushed and turned toward his computer.

Chad was probably right. But what if I changed positions and ended up with one I hated? Blake and I had experienced difficulties in the past, but we worked through our challenges and seemed to be in a good place. To work with Miranda could be a nightmare.

Soon after I returned to my desk, I received an email from her. "I'll be there in a few minutes to talk with you. Reserve the main conference room."

I checked the calendar. The room was no longer available. Miranda arrived before I could find another place to meet. I glanced up from my computer and said, "Chad's in there now."

In a snippy tone she said, "Couldn't you find something else?"

"I was checking when you walked in."

"I think you're doing the right thing to decline the position after all. I'm not sure you're the right person for this job." She spun to leave and spoke aloud to herself. "Can't find an alternate room to meet in."

She hadn't noticed Blake behind her when she stormed out of our office suite.

He rubbed his jaw. "I can't believe she said that to you."

"I know." I tidied up a stack of notes on my desk. "Her actions just now confirmed my decision. I could never work with her, and I think her attitude makes her the prime suspect." I looked back at Blake.

He took a few steps toward me. "Thanks for putting up with all the stuff you have. First me. Then Tauni. Now Miranda. You're an amazing person."

For a few months I referred to Tauni as my nemesis. She succeeded in making my life miserable because I'd become Blake's executive assistant and not her. She experienced a change of heart at a women's conference at Beth's church. A memorable time where Tauni drew closer to the Lord and our friendship sprouted.

Blake took another step closer. "I have a meeting with the finance committee at 2:00. I was informed an hour ago. Are you available to take minutes?"

"In our conference room?" I pointed behind me.

He shook his head. "We're driving over to the chairman of the board's office in his home. We'll leave at 1:40."

When Blake left for lunch, I strolled to the employee lunchroom on the second floor to eat. I finished my meal and sent a text to Jenny's friend, thanked him for the flowers, and told him that I wasn't available.

Blake and I weren't quite a couple yet, and I was uncertain where our relationship was heading, but our friendship was progressing. I needed to put the brakes on to slow things down, although that became more difficult each day.

14

Two

On our drive to the finance committee meeting at Walt Watson's home, I reflected on my new friendship with Blake. He appeared to be ready for romance, but I wasn't sure what the Lord wanted except for me to share hope and God's love with Blake. I didn't think the Lord would approve of more than friendship between the two of us because Blake's relationship with God had soured.

I often prayed for Blake to find his way back to the Lord and to serve God again. In the meantime, I needed to guard my heart. If I remarried, my husband would need to love the Lord with all his heart, soul, mind, and strength as much as my deceased husband, Sam.

We drove through a prestigious neighborhood to Walt Watson's home. Our chairman was a big, snooty man. He reminded me of a cigar-smoking gangster in an old movie. And after seeing the houses in his neighborhood, which must be worth at least three million dollars, I thought the gangster label might fit. We passed through a gate, drove down a long driveway, and stopped in front of a mansion.

"Wow. Is this all one house?"

"Over 10,000 square feet. Quite elaborate. Would you like living in a house like this?"

"I wouldn't want to clean it."

"If you could afford the house, you'd probably hire a cleaning service."

We parked behind three other cars and got out of Blake's dark blue BMW. We hurried up the driveway and climbed a few steps to the front door.

"But why would anyone need to live in a house this big? Do only Walt and his wife live here?"

Blake nodded and rang the doorbell. "You don't like big houses?"

"I don't see the point." I rolled my eyes.

Walt greeted us at the door and welcomed us inside. "Everyone else is here. Let's get started."

Blake followed him into a room to the left of the foyer. Awestruck, I stopped. I stood on marble floor and stared at two staircases. One climbed to my right and the other to my left. I moved forward to get a closer view. The dark wooden spikes and rails were delicately carved swirls. I reached out to touch the smoothness of the wood. I caught sight of an open walkway above me. Fascinating.

"Ms. Reynolds," Walt said. "May we expect your presence anytime soon?"

I rushed to his side—my heels clacking across the floor. "Absolutely beautiful."

"I'm glad you approve." He gave me a single nod.

Blake smiled when I entered the library. The room smelled of books, not at all musty but old. A man's room. A large, dark wooden conference table sat in the center. Walt took a seat at the head, and the others joined him in large brown leather chairs around the table. Except for me. How could I focus on a meeting with all these books? Literature, novels, history, what lurked on these shelves?

"Ms. Reynolds?" Walt said again.

"Sorry." I hurried to an empty chair across from Blake and stared at my notepad.

I took the minutes for a boring meeting and struggled to pay attention. What I wanted to do was tour this house. Although the cost of Walt's home could be better used elsewhere, to help those in need, the place was gorgeous.

After we finished and stood, I glanced at Walt. "May I look around? I feel like I'm in a museum."

He nodded. "Blake, show her the downstairs. You'll need to take her to your place next if she hasn't been there. I suppose she hasn't if she's in awe of my little abode."

My jaw slackened, and I peered at Blake. "You live in a mansion too?"

He hesitated. "I don't think of my home as a mansion. Would you like a tour?"

Now? Alone with him in his house? "Not today." I rubbed my bottom lip. "I guess we should get back to the office. I have a lot to do." I exited the library with Blake close behind.

Walt frowned and stopped me when I moved toward the front door. He told me about the upcoming holiday party for the executive team and board members on December 15 to be held here in his home. He asked me to make the arrangements for forty to fifty people and said I would need to be the hostess since his wife would not be available.

He'd requested another administrative assistant's help a few weeks before, but Alicia, Walt's niece, notified him yesterday she wouldn't have time because of exams and graduation. Miranda wanted me to select Alicia to take my current position when I moved into my new role—the one I no longer wanted.

I tried to keep my composure, but this didn't sit well with me. Only four weeks before the party, and there was much to be done.

"Walt. I'm happy to work on this. I'll need Alicia's help and ask Beth to help too. But I'm busy that evening. I'll see if one of them can be the hostess."

The committee members who remained inside, stopped talking. Blake whispered in my ear, "You can't say no to Walt. I recommend you change your plans."

"Ms. Reynolds. If I wanted Beth, I would have requested her." Walt's tone became indignant. "I didn't. Become available."

Blake placed his hand on my elbow and glanced at Walt. "We better leave now and get these plans in motion. The evening will be wonderful."

He ushered me out the door. "Can't you rearrange your schedule?"

"No. Remember? It's my granddaughter, Nicki's, birthday." I'd told Blake about our family's Grand Ole Opry plans while we were at the conference in New Mexico.

"But Walt wants you. Consider his request an honor."

"Honor? I'm not his wife. Why does he think this is my responsibility? When did his poor planning become my emergency?"

When we reached his car, Blake opened the passenger door. "I know the timing isn't great." He spoke tenderly. "But I'd like you there too." He closed my door, strode to the driver's side, and climbed in.

"Could you attend the Opry on Friday instead? I know someone there who could possibly swap out your tickets for me."

"I can't change the Opry date. Scotty Nelson won't be singing on Friday. He's one of Nicki's favorite performers. Besides, Walt frightens me. I don't like the way he looks at me."

"What?" Blake gawked at me.

"I don't trust him. I don't want to be anywhere alone with him."

"You think he might make a pass at you?"

"Let's say he gives me the creeps." I shuddered and peered at Blake. "Tell me about your house. Larger than Walt's?"

He started his car and drove out into the street. "Not the house. I have more land. Do you have something against large homes?"

"I guess I don't understand. Seems wasteful. Unless you have lots of kids. I'm sure Nicki would love to play hide-and-seek in a house that big."

"Could you see yourself living in a home that size someday?"

My heart pounded in my chest. *Here we go again.* I wanted to go at a snail's pace, and he was thinking about marriage. I blew out a long breath. I could see I needed clarity from the Lord about moving forward with Blake or keeping him at bay.

"I'd get lost. Too much house for me." *Let's nip this now.* "I'd prefer something smaller. A lot smaller."

"Did I tell you about the youth groups we hosted? Or the families we took in with no place to turn after eviction. There were also several battered women and their children. Our home served as the hands and feet of

Jesus more than once over the years."

He appeared lost in thought and didn't notice me as I watched him.

I reached over and quickly touched his arm. "That's a kind and loving reason to have a large home. To help others. Now I feel bad for criticizing your house."

Blake spoke in a soft and wistful tone. "My wife's . . . Cheryl's ministry—to help the hurting and offer them hope."

He offered his hand. I hesitated at first but gave in. He brushed his thumb across mine. *This can't be good.*

I took a couple of deep breaths to calm my anxious thoughts. "What about Walt? I don't want to play hostess. I can't."

"I'll talk to him. He could demand your termination for insubordination. He played an important part in the decision to fire the former VP in Legal. But we have a good relationship. I'll see what I can do."

"Demand my termination?" I raised my voice. "How can he do that? I know he's the chairman of the board, but how can he order me around?"

Calmly Blake said, "Let's say, I wouldn't put the thought past him."

"Well, he better keep his eyes in his head."

"If he does anything inappropriate, tell me." His tone intensified. "I'll get him to stop."

My protector. I probably blushed.

Back at the office I stopped in to see Alicia and Beth. I asked them both for help and to meet me the following morning to discuss our strategy for the holiday party. Beth was eager to assist. Alicia made several excuses but finally said she would stop by before going to class. And to think Miranda wanted me to select her to be our assistant if I'd accepted the promotion. Would be easier to do my job and hers than to have her in our office taking up space.

~

The next morning, a Tuesday, the three of us met in the conference room. I asked Alicia what she'd accomplished since getting the assignment from Walt. She gave me a blank stare and said she didn't have time to do anything.

I read my list of to-dos: order tables and chairs, secure decorations and tablecloths, hire entertainment, prepare a tentative menu, and locate a caterer. Alicia added a live band with a singer, dancing, and a fully stocked bar.

Not a bar. My stomach ached with thoughts of my Aunt Mary in her drunken condition. I lived with her for a few of my teenage years. After my parents died, she turned into an alcoholic.

I asked Alicia to work on the bar and to secure a caterer. Beth took decorations. I offered to locate tables and chairs and the entertainment. Alicia suggested Cindy Walker's band.

Beth caught my eye. "Why not check with Tauni. She knows someone at the Opry. Maybe she can help."

"Great. I'll talk to her." I looked from Beth to Alicia. "Drop by tomorrow morning and let me know what you've been able to accomplish. If you run into any snags, let me know before then."

After Alicia stepped out, I asked Beth, "Why did you avoid the Cindy Walker band?"

"Did I?"

"You gave a slight shake of your head. Who is

she?"

"Cindy's fine, but her mom? Hire Cindy—get Eliza too. Think Jezebel. She'd love to get her hands on Blake. And if you thought Tauni was trouble, Eliza can outdo her 100 times over."

I opened my eyes wide.

I spent most of the morning calling friends from church along with Jenny and Blake's daughter, Allison, to see if they knew anyone to recommend for entertainment. I also checked with Tauni, who offered to help us in any way she could. I came up empty except for a swing band who recently added Christmas songs to their repertoire. Hopefully, Walt liked big bands and wasn't set on having a singer. Maybe they would enjoy a sing-along as a group.

Beth was able to get tables and chairs from her church, so I didn't need to bother with those. She also secured decorations and volunteered to set everything up with Alicia's help on the day of the party. I offered to assist if they got started early that morning.

Wes stopped by to see if we were still on for lunch.

I enjoyed lunches with him. I liked that he didn't put demands on me. "I'll meet you in the lobby in five minutes."

Every time we got together for lunch, I remembered the comment Tauni made at the women's conference a month earlier. She implied Wes thought we were dating, and I should break the news to him gently that we were not. I hadn't seen any indication of affection on his part—only friendship. Tauni was mistaken.

We drove to a nearby café, ordered salads at the counter, and sat near windows overlooking a patio that would be inviting if it were warmer. While we ate, we talked about our Thanksgiving plans. Wes told me that he was going to join his daughter and her husband for dinner.

"I'm cooking this year," I said. "Nicki, Jenny, and her husband, Carl, are coming over."

I hesitated to tell him about Blake, but Wes was a friend. I could trust him. "I invited Blake to join us since his daughter is spending the day with her husband's family."

"Blake? Nice of you." He glanced over at the door of the café and spoke in a serious tone. "There's something I need to tell you."

"What?"

He peered across the restaurant. "I'm dating someone. We're getting close. I feel our lunches should stop."

I nodded. "I understand."

I didn't understand, though. We were having lunch together as friends. I wasn't a threat to their relationship. Was I? Maybe she worked with us. That would possibly explain it.

"Do I know her?"

He fidgeted. "No. But I don't want her to get the wrong idea and become jealous."

I wouldn't want to do anything to interfere with their relationship. He should know that about me. But he didn't seem happy to be dating her. *What's going on here?*

~

I became concerned Wednesday when I hadn't heard from Alicia by noon. When I checked in with her after lunch the day before, she said she was busy and hadn't been able to call the caterers. She promised to come into the office first thing to make calls since classes were finished for the holiday.

The following day was Thanksgiving, and since I planned to take Friday off, too, my morning was hectic. I didn't check with Alicia until after lunch. She apologized but told me that she'd been too busy. She hadn't done anything. Nothing. I should have expected as much.

"Alicia, I was counting on you." I sighed. "I'll take care of it. Please remember you offered to work on December 15 and possibly be hostess at the party."

"I won't be hostess. Uncle Walt said Blake got Eliza Walker since you refused."

Jezebel? Why would Blake ask her? This can't be good.

I spent all afternoon on calls to caterers. Five no answers, three voicemails, and fifteen already booked.

"I'll call those eight again on Friday from home. I may need a Plan B." I spoke out loud to myself.

Beth strolled in. "Plan B for what?"

"We haven't found a caterer yet."

"We?"

"I'm checking. Alicia was too busy."

Beth gasped.

"And she also told me Blake asked Eliza to play hostess for the party."

Beth scrunched up her face. "That's too bad. You may want to change your plans if you're interested in him at all. Eliza is nothing but trouble for Blake."

"This is an important day for Nicki. I'll have to take my chances."

"I warned you." She stepped away.

How bad can Eliza be for Blake? He's a big boy. I'm sure he can take care of himself.

I made my way into his office. "I'm leaving now. Jenny and Carl should arrive tomorrow around 1:30. You're welcome to arrive any time before 2:00 when dinner will be served."

"What time's breakfast?" He grinned.

"Please don't arrive before noon. I won't be ready for guests until then."

"I know my way around a kitchen. I'd love to help."

"That won't be necessary. I'll see you tomorrow afternoon." I hurried out without giving him a chance to say anything more. He'd be a distraction for sure.

On my way home, I stopped by the grocery store and picked up a few items. I hoped Blake would like my dinner. But why did I feel that I needed to make this dinner more elaborate? Didn't make sense. I didn't need to win him over. He was already smitten with me.

Three

My doorbell rang at 11:45 a.m. I closed the oven and removed my hand mitt. *Blake.* Couldn't he wait fifteen more minutes? I was glad everything was either in the oven or prepped, and the table was set. I strolled through the living room prepared to greet Blake. But there on my porch stood Wes in jeans and a plaid flannel shirt. "This is a surprise."

"I hoped you were alone. Has anyone arrived yet?"

I cocked my head. "What's up?"

"May we talk? I won't take long."

"Of course. Come in." I pointed to the couch. "Have a seat."

A line appeared between his eyebrows.

"What's wrong?" I sat across from him. "Are you ill?"

He shook his head and stood. His gaze darted toward the door and back at me. "Nothing like that." He ran his hand through his dark hair. "Is there any chance for us?"

My heart felt like it hit the floor. "Us? What happened to your girlfriend?" I stammered. "I don't understand."

He turned his head away. "No girlfriend. I made up that story. I'm here to come clean with you and not wait until Monday." He sat again on the sofa.

I spoke in a gentle tone. "What's going on?"

Wes focused on the floor. "I planned at lunch on Tuesday to ask you out for a real date. Dinner, dancing, movie, whatever." He shuffled his feet. "When you mentioned Blake . . ." He looked up at me and swallowed hard. "I saw a gleam in your eye that wasn't there two months ago. I should have made my intentions known sooner." He shook his head. "Better you know the truth."

Movement outside my front window caught my eye.

When the doorbell rang, Wes stood. "I'll leave. Do you have a back door?"

"Not necessary. I'm sorry we won't be able to talk about this now. Could we meet for coffee tomorrow afternoon or evening?"

"Sure."

I opened the door, and Wes slipped past Blake, who sported a startled look. "I was just leaving. Happy Thanksgiving to you both."

Blake took a step back. "Wes? Happy Thanksgiving." He narrowed his eyes and searched my face. "What was he doing here?"

"He needed to talk." I held the door open for Blake and he stepped inside. "He's struggling with something right now."

Blake glanced out the door toward Wes's pickup, watched as he pulled away, and peered at me. "He's just a friend, right?"

I nodded. "Just a friend."

"And I'm just a friend too?"

My smile grew. "I suppose we can replace the word 'just' with 'special' for you since I hold your hand."

Blake took my hand, brought it to his lips, and kissed my fingers. "I have something for you in the car. I'll be right back." He stepped outside and jogged to his car. He returned with a bouquet of lavender and dark purple roses in a floral etched glass vase. He sent me roses a few times over the past two months. Beautiful bouquets with handwritten cards that expressed the colors' meanings.

I brought my hands together in front of my face and rested them on my chin. "Stunning. Absolutely breathtaking. What do they mean?"

He frowned. "Mean? What are you asking? They don't mean anything, do they?"

"You know good and well they do." I playfully slugged his arm.

"Read the card and see if you can figure out what purple means."

I tore open the envelope and read his message. The card mentioned the first time we met. "What? Does purple mean trouble or elevator doors closing in my face?" He told me last weekend that when he first saw me, he knew I'd be trouble. But when we met face to face, we were standing in front of the elevator.

He winked. "Maybe Nicki can figure out the meaning. Ask her when she gets here."

"That's not fair. She's five." I scanned the living room. "Where's my phone? I'll look up the meaning."

The oven timer beeped in the kitchen. "Would you put the bouquet in the TV room?" I pointed down the hall. "First door on the right. Use the side table next to the sofa. I'm sure we'll all spend time in there today and enjoy them together."

I forgot the purple flowers for a while. After I tended to our dinner, I sat next to Blake on the couch in the living room. "Tell me about Eliza Walker. I understand you asked her to play hostess at the party."

"Did you secure her daughter's band?"

I shook my head. "I haven't contacted them. Are they available?"

"They had a cancellation. Walt will want them."

"I secured a swing band. They're amazing."

He wrinkled his nose. "I think a swing band, with the Walker band available, will get you fired quicker than you not being hostess at the party."

"I'll call her tomorrow." I sighed and nudged his arm with my elbow. "Tell me about Eliza."

"What have you heard?"

"Why are you being sly with me?"

"I'm not sly. A little mischievous, perhaps." He grinned.

"What I heard wasn't complimentary. How do you know her? What is she like?"

He took my hand. "I haven't seen her in a few years. She hung around a lot when Cheryl died. They were friends. Cheryl loved people and saw the good in them, even when their character was questionable. I loved that side of her, along with her tenderness and compassion, but she misjudged Eliza." He rubbed the back of his head. "Eliza took on the role of comforter for me. I soon realized she was more interested in Cheryl's husband than she was in Cheryl's passing."

"Oh?" My voice cracked.

He turned my chin toward him and peered into my eyes. "You don't need to be concerned. She's not my type."

"Did I say I was concerned?"

"You didn't have to. I'm learning to read you well."

I couldn't let this slip by. I wasn't over last weekend's turn-of-events. When Blake first found his son in Albuquerque, Andy didn't want anything to do with his dad. Blake ended up in the hotel bar with a young woman named Brandi. Although he'd assured me there was nothing between the two of them and drinking was not his normal way of dealing with problems, I struggled with this news concerning Eliza. "Why would you call her knowing what you just told me?"

He avoided my eyes. "Walt insisted."

I nodded, bit my lip, and stared at our clasped hands. "This reminds me of Brandi all over again."

In Albuquerque, I had this crazy idea Blake would try to woo me with romance at a dinner banquet because he'd been attentive and sweet. But he drank too much that evening and spent his time with Brandi. The next day, he apologized and promised me a romantic do-over evening.

He let go of my hand, scooted toward me, and placed his arm across my shoulders. He leaned closer and kissed my cheek. "She meant nothing to me. You know that."

We were too close. *Can't do this.* I stood and peered at him. "But now you've asked Eliza to be hostess." Frustration crept into my words. "You tell me not to be concerned, but I am. She has a reputation."

Blake stood. "I will see her one night. I did it to keep peace with Walt, so you could keep your job. There's nothing between Eliza and me. Never will be."

I gazed deep into his eyes. I wanted to believe him.

"Stop looking at me like that. This isn't the romantic setting I'm going for." The corners of his eyes crinkled. "You won't have to wait long."

I'm sure I blushed. "I need to check on dinner." *How did I look at him? Pull yourself together Keedryn. You're getting soft. Lord, take control.*

~

I was relieved when Jenny, Carl, and Nicki arrived early.

Nicki ran to me and wrapped her arms around my legs. "Nana. I missed you."

I knelt to give her a bear hug. She gaped up at Blake and whispered in my ear. "He's cute like you said."

She peeked up at Blake again. "Did you bring roses today?"

"I did. They're in the TV room." He caught me eyeing him and offered a bemused smile. "Let me know what you think?"

She ran out of sight, and I introduced Blake to Jenny and Carl. They shook hands and talked about the weather and football. The men headed toward the TV room, while Jenny and I made our way into the kitchen.

Nicki came running to me. "Can I have your phone? I don't know what purple means."

I took my cell off the kitchen counter and gave it to her. "I haven't searched. Have Mommy help you."

Jenny helped Nicki find a website that described the meaning of each rose color.

"Read it, Mommy."

Jenny looked at Nicki. "Enchantment."

Nicki's mouth twisted. "What does that mean?"

Jenny shrugged. "That's a hard one to describe. Let's say to like something a lot." She lowered her voice. "Also says, 'Love at first sight.' Mom?"

I pulled the card from my pocket and now understood the meaning. I gave the card to Jenny.

She read it out loud. "I remember the first time I saw you." She whispered loudly. "He's declaring his love for you. He's the hottest old guy I've ever seen. Don't let him get away."

"Shh. Your daughter can hear you." I frowned. "Goodness. Blake and Carl probably heard you too." I tapped my finger on the countertop. "Love at first sight doesn't literally mean love at first sight, silly. Only means he was attracted to me when he first saw me, and he told me that in Albuquerque."

"Really? And you didn't tell me? Any other secrets?" Jenny shoved my arm. "Blake must love roses. Do you know why they're special to him?"

"His daughter, Allison, told me when we first met that her mom grew them. Each family member became an expert in their care and color meanings."

"Doesn't it bother you that Blake gives you the same flower that his wife loved?"

"Not at all. Allison said that until my birthday in September he hadn't had anything to do with roses since her mom's death. She believed that when he gave me the flowers, he'd taken a huge step because he was sharing a part of himself with me."

"Sounds like you're special to him too."

I pulled Jenny toward the window overlooking my

back yard. I didn't want to be overheard by Blake. "To him roses represent many beautiful qualities. I'm sure if I told him another flower was my favorite, he'd give me those instead. But I'm honored to be the first person in over five years that he's cared enough for to share his thoughts and feelings with this way."

"Wow, Mom. I think he does love you." She took a grinning Nicki by the hand. "Let's wash up for dinner."

They scurried away, and I could hear Nicki. "He does loves Nana, doesn't he?"

I hoped Blake didn't hear her but knew he probably did since Jenny and Nicki passed the TV room to get to the bathroom.

When Jenny and Nicki returned, Carl and Blake trailed behind them into the kitchen. We gathered in a circle and held hands. Carl asked Blake if he'd like to say the blessing.

Blake's eyes darted around the circle. He bowed his head, and we followed suit. He prayed a short prayer of thanksgiving.

Lunch was served family buffet style. We lined up to fill our plates with turkey, dressing, mashed potatoes, sweet potato casserole, and other holiday standards. Jenny was first and filled a small plate with Nicki's favorites. I was next in line followed by Blake and Carl.

Nicki scampered over and hugged Blake's legs. When he gazed at her, she glanced up and beamed. "Jesus liked your prayer."

Such a sweet disposition.

Blake patted her head. "Did you find out what purple means?

"Yes. Papa Blake."

I whirled to face her. My eyes bulged. "Nicki." I

was ready to send her to my room with a good scolding.

She hid behind Blake's legs and peeked out. Tears filled her eyes. "I'm sorry, Nana." She peered back up at Blake and pulled away from his legs. She sniffled. "Yes. Mr. Blake. Purple means you want Nana to love you like you love her."

My jaw dropped open. "Nicki." She stared at me with a pouty face. Jenny put her plate on the table and took Nicki by the hand. They scurried down the hallway. I couldn't look at Blake. I wanted to crawl into a corner. With a shaky hand, I filled my plate.

Blake nudged my elbow. "You warned me about her."

I had when I first invited him to dinner. And she certainly delivered with her embarrassing remark. I raised my eyes to meet his and gave him a sheepish expression.

"You were right." He chuckled. "Feisty one she is. Don't let what she said upset you. She's precious. A lot like her Nana."

"Feisty or precious?" The twinkle in his eye told me for sure feisty.

We both neared the end of the line. I gawked when I saw Blake's overflowing plate. "Do you have everything you need? Perhaps you'd like to use a platter instead?"

Jenny and Nicki returned to the kitchen. Nicki ran to the table and sat. Jenny got in line behind Carl.

Blake leaned toward me. "I'm good. May I sit with you?"

My table seats four. Too crowded to pull in another chair. I was grateful Carl and Jenny offered to eat in the TV room.

"I plan to sit here at the table with Nicki. Wouldn't you rather watch the game?"

He narrowed his eyes. "I think getting to know Nicki better will be much more entertaining."

During dinner, Nicki rambled on about her favorite songs and movies, Kindergarten, friends from church and school, and her imaginary pet turtle, Tiny. Fortunately, Tiny stays outdoors most of the time because he causes a lot of mischief. Blake appeared enthralled with her stories. Either that or he was a good sport.

~

After dinner, the men watched football while Jenny and I cleaned the kitchen. Blake offered to help, but my kitchen was too small for three. Nicki ran off to look for my orange tabby. She and Jenny took care of Roxie while I was in Albuquerque, and Nicki made it a game to find my cat's hiding places.

With the kitchen now tidy, I strolled to the TV room and was stunned to see Nicki in Blake's lap reading to him. He gave her his undivided attention. He seemed to enjoy Nicki more than the game. She was usually shy when she met someone for the first time. Her immediate fondness toward Blake caught me by surprise.

Jenny stood close and whispered, "He's charming. He's nothing like what you described a few months ago. He'd be good for you. You know that, don't you?"

I followed her back to the kitchen and told her about the flowers I'd received from Dan, her friend from church. I spoke in a hushed tone. "Something also happened before you came over that complicates things. I'm not sure how to handle the situation." I told Jenny about my conversation with Wes.

"Blake, Dan, and Wes. You have your pick. And the winner is?" She flung her hands out and up. A ta-dah moment.

I stared at her with a blank face. "This is serious."

Her grin disappeared. "What did you tell Wes?"

"Nothing. Blake came to the door before I could respond."

"I know you. You'll pray, and the Lord will direct you on how you should answer him." She shoved me in a playful way. "Are we ready to play Spades?"

Jenny loved cards and thrived on competition. We slid into the TV room. "Can you guys tear yourselves away from the game to play Spades? A Reynolds family tradition." Jenny's eyes grew large.

Blake stood and sat Nicki on the floor with her book. "Spades? I'm undefeated."

I reached out my hand. "You're my teammate."

While we played at the kitchen table, Nicki watched her favorite Disney movie of all time—*Frozen.*

Blake's eyes lit up whenever he could hear her sing. Occasionally, when a hand was dealt, he'd go into the TV room to pay her a visit. One time, I followed him.

He squatted next to her where she sat on the floor. "How many times have you seen this movie? You know all of the songs and sing beautifully."

"A bunch Pa—ah, Mr. Blake." She spotted me with my hands on my hips behind him.

We finished our card game, and I complimented Blake on his continued winning streak.

Jenny's not a gracious loser. She hung her head, stood, and shuffled to the fridge. She pulled out a plate of leftovers she'd prepared earlier and called to Nicki to let her know they needed to go home. When Jenny opened the front door, Nicki ran to Blake. He knelt and hugged her goodbye. She whispered in his ear and ran over and cuddled me.

After they left, Blake took my hand, and we stood face to face.

"Nicki found a new friend today," I said. "Usually takes her longer to warm up to people."

"She's a good judge of character."

"She always has been." I tilted my head. "What did she whisper to you?"

His eyes glowed. "Don't get mad at her now. She said, 'I love you, Papa Blake.'"

I shook my head. "I don't know where she came up with that. She got the idea in her head with the first bouquet. She won't let it go."

"She's adorable. I wouldn't change a thing." He took my other hand. "She made my day. And you made me a part of your family tradition."

I warmed at his touch. I was falling hard and didn't know what to do with my emotions. This could become a nightmare. *Falling in love with my boss? What was I thinking? What am I doing?* I exhaled a deep breath. "I did do that, didn't I?"

"And in nine days, you'll be joining one of my family's traditions. Although it's been five years, I'm pleased you will be with us when we welcome the Christmas season with a family dinner the first weekend in December."

"I'm looking forward to it. Too bad Andy won't be here to celebrate with us."

Blake nodded and moved closer still holding both

of my hands. "Your daughter's lovely, like her mother. And she's smart too. And Nicki's pretty smart."

"Smart? Why do you say that?"

"They seem to understand roses better than you do. They both understood the color well."

His blue eyes pierced my soul. I pulled my right hand away from his and pointed to the couch. My legs felt weak.

"I can't stay. I want to take you in my arms and kiss you." He pushed a strand of hair behind my ear.

My heart raced. I wet my lips, took one step closer, and whispered, "I give you permission."

He leaned toward me, and I closed my eyes. I felt his lips—they grazed the top of my head. I took a step back and squinted at him. Such a letdown. I pulled my other hand away from his and looked down so I could breathe and calm my heart.

Blake tenderly touched my chin and lifted my face toward him. "Not yet. Your home is lovely, but I have something else planned for you." He again took my hand in his. "Nicki whispered something else."

I raised my eyebrows.

"Jesus loves you too." His eyes glistened.

I nodded. "She has a tender heart for the Lord."

He kissed me on the cheek and opened the door. "May I call you tomorrow? Maybe we could get together for lunch or dinner."

"We talked about lunch after church on Sunday. Does that still work for you?" On our drive to the airport to fly home from the conference, Blake agreed to attend church with me and have lunch together afterward.

"I'll see you Sunday morning." He stepped outside

and strode to his car.

From my open doorway, I called out to him. "Blake." He turned my way. "He does love you."

He smiled and waved.

I pushed the door closed, leaned my back against it, and let out a long breath. "And so do I."

Four

Although today was Black Friday and the office was closed, the holiday party demanded my attention. There was much to do with the bash three weeks away. I contacted Cindy Walker, and she confirmed her band was available.

I was unsuccessful in securing a caterer. *May need to cook this meal myself.* I gave a resigned sigh and slumped into my chair with no idea how to pull that off. Thanksgiving and Christmas were a stretch for me—cooking for four or five.

Jenny called. I told her about the holiday party dilemma and asked if I could borrow her smoker on December 15. She suggested we ask our churches to get involved. Both churches offered mid-week meals and excellent cooks. We discussed the menu which included brisket, pulled pork, sausage, and chicken. Jenny offered to make calls to see if we could pull everything together.

"Do you think Blake would let us use his kitchen?" She squealed with excitement in her voice. "I imagine there's plenty of room if his house is huge."

"Why? The cooks can prepare everything at their churches, can't they?"

"Possibly. But I think it will be better and more fun to be all together."

"I'll ask. He'll probably want us to use the chairman of the board's kitchen since the party will be held there. I'll call you back later."

We ended our call. *Fun? She must be kidding. This was torture.* Alicia should have asked for my help when Walt first asked her to organize the party.

I sat at my kitchen table and clicked on Blake's number. He sounded happy when he answered my call and agreed to us using our churches' cooks.

Before I plowed ahead with my next question, I said a short prayer. I asked if we could use his kitchen as our home base. "Our churches have commercial food warmers and vans we can borrow to transport the food to Walt's."

"That doesn't make sense because the party will be at Walt's. Plan to do everything there."

My gut twisted. "But I'm not comfortable being in Walt's house."

When Blake realized I would spend the day assisting the cooks and organizing people and tasks, he softened to the idea but told me that his chef wouldn't be available to help.

His chef? I had no idea.

Since I needed to leave by 5:00 p.m. to make it to the Grand Ole Opry for Nicki's birthday, Blake suggested I call Allison. If she were available to help supervise the kitchen at his house and if Beth could oversee BCH staff with the setup at Walt's, we'd have his approval.

I felt relieved and thankful that when I saw Blake's house for the first time, there would be a lot of people present helping to get ready for the holiday party. A private tour of his home, alone with him, would make me nervous and may start rumors.

~

I called Allison while I stared out my front window to the condo's parking area. We moved quickly through a lot of topics in a short period of time. Thanksgiving, our upcoming "family dinner," finding Andy, and the holiday party. She was excited to help. She cheerfully agreed to be lead chef and kitchen captain. Near the end of our conversation, she asked if Blake shared the details of her mom's accident with me. I told her no. I still didn't know anything. She sounded as though she wanted to discuss new information with me.

After I finished my conversation with Allison, I called Wes. "Are you available to meet for coffee?"

"Why don't we talk on the phone? I'm feeling a bit under the weather today. I think I ate too much turkey." He sounded down. "Are you and Blake getting serious?"

"I'm not sure what will happen with Blake and me." I moved to the sofa and sat. "But I'd decided to pursue a deeper friendship with him before you stopped by yesterday."

"I'm okay with you dating both of us. What do you think about that?"

Help me, Lord. "I'm sorry, Wes, I've cherished our time together, but I don't believe that will work." I moved my cell to my left ear.

"So, you won't give me a chance?"

"You've been a blessing to me, and I've enjoyed our friendship. But that's all it can be."

"Oh, I see. Thanks."

He hung up. I hurt him. Me—the bad guy. Not something I enjoyed. I'd miss our time together. When did life become so complicated? I broke two men's hearts without dating. Dan and Wes.

Would Blake be number three? *Or will he hurt me? I need to remember to guard my heart.*

~

I refused to make calls on Saturday, and no one called me. No party follow-up. No suitors or potential suitors. A great day, although I missed my Nicki. I hoped to see her again soon.

On Sunday morning I waited inside the main entrance of the church for Blake. I waved and stepped toward him when he entered the lobby. "You look dashing this morning in your brown suede jacket. New?" I reached out to shake his hand.

Blake moved in for a hug. "I missed you yesterday."

I ignored his comment. "Come with me. I want you to meet my small group leader, Manuel. I told you about him when we were in Albuquerque. Remember?" I grabbed Blake's hand, led him across the lobby past an eight-foot tall Christmas tree, and to the education wing. We found Manuel talking with a couple of teen boys in the hallway. I caught his attention and made introductions after the boys entered their classroom. I let go of Blake's hand, so he could shake Manuel's and was surprised by how clammy his palm had become.

After chatting for a few minutes, Blake and I strolled toward the worship center. We were stopped by a few older ladies, who were interested in meeting my new friend.

The worship band was playing an upbeat song

when we entered the sanctuary. We found two seats in the middle of the center section and remained standing. The songs slowed and became more worshipful. I fought tears. Part of my emotion was because Blake stood next to me holding my hand like my husband, Sam, used to do before he died. I could get used to this. The rest of my emotion was because of my thankfulness to the Lord for His blessings and love. When seated, our pastor presented a dynamic message. He challenged us to go deeper in our walk with God.

After the service, several people welcomed Blake. He helped me with my jacket, and we made our way to the parking lot. "A great service. Not what I expected. I see why you enjoy attending here. Uplifting music and powerful preaching."

"You're welcome anytime." I was delighted he enjoyed the service. Maybe this was what he needed to come back to the Lord.

He squeezed my hand, and we talked about lunch. I suggested Cheesecake Factory. We waited a few minutes before the hostess led us to a booth where we sat across from each other and chatted. After our food arrived, Blake mentioned our dinner plans for Saturday.

"Where are we going?" I wanted details.

"A place called Samson's, in Franklin. Have you ever been?"

"I'm not familiar with it."

"Quiet, soft music, private, and intimate." He spoke in a smooth tone. "I think you'll enjoy the atmosphere."

I watched a waiter taking the order from a nearby table. Sounded like a romantic place. Perhaps a good place for a kiss. I wouldn't make that mistake again.

You have my permission. How embarrassing. Besides. He wouldn't kiss me at Samson's with his daughter and her husband present. That would be weird. I eyed Blake. I needed to keep in mind he tended to be sneaky. He'd plant one on me when I least expected it. "I look forward to spending time with your family." Our waitress refilled our water glasses and walked away. "How did Allison take the news regarding Cheryl?"

He peered at the table. "She's upset with me."

"Would you like to discuss her reaction?"

"She's disappointed I didn't tell her sooner." He propped his elbows on the table and massaged his temples. "She's hurt too. She's the one who stuck by my side the entire time. But I told Andy before her." He shook his head. "I'm not ready to go into details yet." He slouched in his seat and stared down at his hands.

I should have kept my mouth shut. I wasn't good at pulling people out of the doldrums. I reached over and touched Blake's hand that now rested on the table. "Did I tell you about Nicki's latest adventure with Tiny?"

That brought a twinkle to his eye.

~

Early Monday morning, before Blake arrived at the office, Tauni came by to see me.

I asked about her holiday. She nodded toward the conference room—available and perfect for private discussions. After we sat next to each other, she lowered her head and told me that she and her boyfriend, Mitch, drove to Birmingham for lunch with his family.

I wrinkled my nose. "Things didn't go well?"

"His family loved me. Especially when they asked if anyone wanted to pray over lunch, and I volunteered." She picked at her fingernails. "Things aren't going well with Mitch. We're struggling. That's why I stopped by to talk with you."

I dipped my head to see her eyes. "How can I help?"

"When Mitch and I started dating, I was the 'old' Tauni. I'm not her anymore. He's not as crazy about the new me." She glanced up. "I need advice and guidance—someone to teach me how to be a godly woman and hold me accountable."

"Are you asking me to be that person?"

"Would you mentor me? I need help with work, God, relationships, and life in general. I'd love to learn from you."

I placed my hand on my chest. "I'm honored you asked. I haven't done anything like this before." I leaned closer to her. "Do you have ideas on how you'd like to get started?"

"Could we meet once a week to chat about life and see where that leads?"

"Sounds good to me."

She smacked her hands together. "Could we start this week?"

I chuckled at her enthusiasm. "How do Wednesdays during our lunch hour sound?"

"Great. I'm excited about this."

"So am I. This will be good for both of us."

Amazing. My former nemesis asked me to mentor her. *God, You are good.*

Blake was near my desk when we returned. He did a double take when he saw Tauni. Her professional attire alone was enough to catch his attention.

She gazed down and back up at him. "I'm sorry

about your presentation. If anyone messed with the slides when I left my desk, I'm fully responsible. I'm now careful to put my monitor in sleep mode before I walk away."

"Sounds like you've taken steps to prevent future problems." He smiled. "Keep up the good work." He took a step toward his office.

Tauni followed. "Wait. I apologized to Keedryn a few weeks ago. I need to say this to you too." She glanced at me and back at Blake. "I came in here more than once …" She paused and looked at the floor. "I was inappropriately dressed and acted foolish and mean." She peered up at Blake again. "I'd like you to know how sorry I am. I'm not that person any longer."

Blake's eyes widened. "What you just did takes courage. Lots of it." He nodded and continued to his office.

After she left, Blake came out of his office and stood in front of my desk. "I believe you're right regarding Tauni. If God can change her heart, maybe there's hope for me too."

~

Beth and I worked together throughout the week to get everything finalized with the churches for the holiday party two weeks from that Saturday. We decided not to include Alicia on anything other than the bar. That became her one responsibility.

Tauni and I met for the first time on Wednesday. We spent our lunch hour chatting about family and work relationships. I was guarded when she questioned me concerning the healthcare conference. I didn't feel it was my place to mention Andy, and I didn't say anything in relation to my growing friendship with

Blake. She talked mostly about her relationship with Mitch, and hopefully I gave her the encouragement she sought.

On Friday at the office, I realized how the week had flown by. Perhaps the most enjoyable week yet working with Blake. He changed a lot since our trip to Albuquerque. He was attentive in a professional way. Not at all demanding. He treated me with full respect. I hoped the change in him meant he was drawing closer to the Lord.

Later that afternoon, Blake came out to my desk and spoke quietly. "Are you all set for tomorrow night at 6:00?"

"This is a fancy place, right?"

"Semi-formal. Kind of classy."

"I may need to visit the mall." I frowned and tapped my finger against my lower lip.

"Call Allison. She might have something. I'd hate to see you spend a lot of money for one night."

I raised my eyebrows and pouted. "Only one night?"

"Not what I meant."

"Oh? You *will* take me to a fancy place again?"

"I will, but you'll have to commit first."

"So, tomorrow night's a teaser?" I tilted my head and pursed my lips.

He shook his head, turned away, and mumbled. "Women."

Five

Early December

On Saturday morning, I contacted Allison and asked if I could borrow a dress for the evening. She was happy to help. We agreed to meet at my place at noon, have lunch, and try on dresses. She brought six with her. Red, three shades of blue, dark pink, and mint green. The colors were gorgeous. A couple of them were cut lower in the bodice than I cared to wear, but each was beautiful. We laid them on the sofa in my living room and hurried through lunch. I was eager to try them on.

"I think this one would be stunning on you. The blue matches Dad's eyes." Allison giggled. "You two would sparkle together."

"I would at least. All these sequins glimmer in the light. I like the three-quarter length sleeves. And it appears the dress is long enough to cover my knobby knees."

"This may be the only one you need to try."

I rushed to my bedroom and carefully got into the dress. I didn't want to damage any of the sequins. I admired myself in my bedroom mirror longer than I should have. Allison showed up a few minutes later.

Her mouth fell open. "The dress for you. You look amazing. Dad will do flips when he sees you."

"Flips? You're too funny."

"Do you have shoes to match?" She made herself at home and rummaged through my closet. "What about these? Slip them on." She tossed a pair of silver strappy sandals toward me.

I put them on and paraded through my room. "What do you think?"

"I think they're perfect." She hugged me and said, "It's still early. What if we redo your makeup and hair? I supported myself through college working at a Clinique counter."

"You supported yourself through college?" *That's hard to believe.*

"Not actually supported. I worked to buy my meals. I hated cafeteria food."

I slipped out of the dress and agreed to a makeover. After an hour of primping, Allison allowed me the privilege of a mirror. I stood and viewed my reflection in the bathroom.

"You're amazing. I'm—"

"Beautiful?"

"I look better than I have in years."

"Actually, you're gorgeous." She stood behind me, placed her hands on my shoulders, and peeked into the mirror. "Dad thinks so too."

I placed my hand on my chest. "That's sweet. But I've never thought of myself that way."

"He does. On Monday at lunch, he talked about you the entire time. He said, 'I don't think I've seen a more beautiful woman since your mom.'" She turned me to face her. "He's crazy about you." She pulled her cell out of her pocket. "Put the dress back on and let me take your picture. Dad will want a copy for sure." She led me back into my bedroom and helped me into the dress. "Smile." She snapped the picture and texted me a copy.

"How am I going to keep this fresh appearance for three more hours? Everything may wear off before he picks me up. I might wilt during the evening and turn into a pumpkin."

She giggled. "I think you have the story a little mixed up. You're worried over nothing. You'll still be beautiful to Dad when he arrives at 6:00. Trust me." She got quiet. "Has he told you yet about Mom?"

I shook my head. "He's not ready. I don't want to push. Can you forgive him?"

"I have. The Lord's forgiven me plenty." She gazed at the ceiling. "I'm hurt and grieving all over again." She peered at me. "I've asked for her journals, but he won't budge."

"Has he read them?"

"He can't. They're too painful. Would you ask him?"

I took a step back. "Since I'm not family, I think the two of you should work this out. I'll be praying."

Her frown quickly turned to another giggle. "I've got a great idea. You should call Dad and tell him that you're coming to the restaurant with Jim and me. That way, I can see his face when he first sees you."

Allison's excitement was contagious. We agreed I would ask Blake. I was surprised when we strolled into the living room and she sat on the couch. I expected she'd want to get home to primp. I sat across from her in my big comfy rocker. She told me that she expected great things for tonight because she enjoyed watching couples in love.

"You're carrying this way out of proportion," I said.

"I disagree. You're in for a real treat tonight. Dad shared a few things with me. He's worked hard to make this a special night for you."

"Now, you've got me scared."

"He won't propose if that's why you're concerned."

"Propose?" My eyes nearly popped out of my head. "We're not even dating."

"Whatever you say." Her smile faded. "I need to share something with you before I go. Not sure if now's the best time. But I'd like to tell you about a dream from a couple of months ago."

"A dream?"

"I don't have many, but this one seemed real." She bit at her lip. "I saw a stunning woman dressed for her wedding day. She carried a bouquet of roses. Her dress, though not a typical wedding gown, was magnificent. Delicately woven deep purple lace covered a lavender lining."

"Deep purple and lavender?" My heart raced. "Those were the colors in the bouquet he brought me on Thanksgiving Day." I jumped up. "Allison . . ."

"You do know that those mean 'love at first sight,' don't you? Why are you surprised regarding any of this? The roses? My dream? I told you before that he's crazy about you." She motioned for me to sit and her tone turned soft. "Please allow me to finish."

I sat and gave her my full attention.

"The bride radiated confidence and love and held herself like a queen. The groom was my dad. I didn't get a clear look at his bride's face until she arrived at the front where I stood." She teared up. "You were his bride. The dream occurred the night before we met. I came to the office to see if you were the woman. Do you remember my gasp when the elevator doors opened?"

I stood, pulled my hair behind my ears, and trudged to the kitchen.

Allison came up behind me. "Dad had spoken about you with fondness, and I believed it would be you. I don't mean to scare you or make you uncomfortable, but please be open to whatever the Lord asks of you."

I turned to face her. "Your dad will need to have a change of heart with regards to the Lord before I could ever consider marriage."

"Please give him time—as much as he needs. I wouldn't ask you to compromise what you believe, but he's an incredible man."

"I agree." I touched her upper arm. "He is."

Her face beamed. "I've got to get home, do my hair and makeup, and change. We'll be back at 6:00 to pick you up." She hugged me again before she left.

I immediately called Blake. "What are your plans for tonight? Allison was here with the dresses. She sounded like something special would take place."

He chuckled. "We'll enjoy a lovely dinner, and I hope to show my *special friend* how much I appreciate and admire her." He spoke in an animated tone. "Give me a chance. I think you'll be pleased."

"I'd like to meet you there." I sighed. "Allison and Jim want to pick me up."

"Why?"

"Allison thought it'd be fun."

"That's not what I planned." He sounded grumpy.

"May help smooth things over between you two."

"Will I have the honor of taking you home?"

"Yes."

"Then I'm okay."

"That will make Allison happy. I'll meet you there at 6:30."

~

Allison squealed with excitement when she arrived. "You look amazing."

"You've already seen me."

"But Daddy hasn't. He's going to be blown away."

"Daddy?"

"I call him Daddy when I get excited. This will be a night out of a fairy tale."

"I hope the story doesn't include a wicked witch."

"Not at all. You'll be treated like a royal princess. Shall we go? Our carriage awaits."

Outside, Jim stood next to his Ford Escape and played the part of a chauffeur opening the two passenger doors. Allison made quick introductions and directed me to the front, and she sat in the back. We hurried off to the restaurant and commented on the Christmas lights we passed.

All the nervousness I'd carried throughout the day vanished with Jim in the car. His humor kept me on my toes. However, I wasn't sure when he was serious or joking. We seemed to disagree on yard decorations when we passed through one upscale neighborhood.

What he described as tasteful, I thought to be horrid. I think he liked to tease.

When we pulled into the restaurant's parking lot, we were greeted by a valet wearing a Santa hat.

Inside, I led the way to Blake and our table. The restaurant was elegantly decorated with fine linen tablecloths, fresh flower centerpieces, and soft lighting casting romantic, alluring shadows throughout. The instrumental Christmas music playing through the speaker system gave a calm and soothing affect.

My focus, however, was the handsome man in the dark blue jacket. He stood with his hands clasped behind his body. His entire face glowed. He peered at me like I was the only woman in the room. He took both of my hands in his and gazed deep into my eyes. "I've anticipated this moment all day. You are ravishing."

My knees weakened. "You look mighty fine yourself. Your stubble—going for a rugged appearance?"

"Often on weekends. Do you like?"

I gently cupped my hand on his cheek. Although the stubble was prickly, I noticed my touch was well-received. My eyes remained on his. "I do. Very much."

"Hey you two. You have chairs." Jim's voice echoed in the distance. "Can you quit staring and sit? I'm starving and want to order."

I noticed Allison across the table. Her eyes were big and round.

Blake pulled out my chair and gawked at Jim. "Sorry."

We took our seats, and I glanced at Blake. My heart almost jumped out of my chest. *This is a date. A real date. I should fake a headache and ask Allison to drive me home.*

Blake pointed to the opposite side of me.

"I'm sorry." I grabbed a menu from the waiter and flipped it open.

Blake leaned close to my ear. "Sparks."

I wrinkled my forehead and squinted. "Stop."

Allison kept her eyes on us. "What did you say to her? Sparks? By the expression on her face, she's ready to smack you."

Blake grinned. "Keedryn has a little habit I picked up on. She likes to stare at me. Her eyes light up like the night sky and sparks fly." He made an overly dramatic wave of his hands.

I pursed my lips. "Mr. Conner. You flatter yourself a little too much."

"Be nice, Dad."

Sweet of Allison to come to my defense.

We placed our dinner orders, and I excused myself to the Ladies Room to wash my hands. Allison followed. Times hadn't changed. Women still liked to go to the powder room together.

Inside the restroom, I strolled to the sink. Allison whispered, "What happened between the two of you out there?"

"What do you mean?" I turned on the water, pumped the soap dispenser, and washed my hands.

She spoke to my reflection in the mirror. "Your eyes and smiles while you gazed at each other. Like wow. Jim tried to get your attention three times before you two responded."

I could see my face turn red. "I guess we both got caught up in the moment. No big deal." I reached for a paper towel.

"No big deal? Are you crazy? You cannot deny his attraction or yours."

"You seem to be handling the time with your dad well. Did the two of you talk again after you left my house?"

She looked at the floor. "No. This is a special night. We haven't held this family tradition in years. You're here with us. Dad's becoming Dad again. I don't want to do anything to mess that up." She tapped her heel up and down on the floor. "Although I'm upset with him, I love him bunches."

I spun and faced Allison. "Did you hear what you just said?"

She jerked her head up. "What? I love him bunches?"

"You said Dad is becoming Dad again. Ever since your mother died, he stopped being the dad you knew. This different dad couldn't see why not telling you the full truth could hurt you more." I tossed my paper towel into the trash. "He's now becoming the dad you remember growing up. Your mother's death hurt him deeply. Changed him. He no longer processed things the same way."

"You may be right. I need to stop punishing him." She appeared serious for a moment before she gave me a playful shove. "You tried to avoid my comment a moment ago. You can't deny what happened out there. No doubt Dad loves you, and you're in love with him too."

Six

What was I going to do? Allison was right. The way Blake gazed into my eyes, his smiles, and attention, he loved me. That I couldn't deny. And I him, but I can't. This wasn't supposed to happen. *Lord, You told me to share Your love, not mine. I'm a goner. So much for guarding my heart.*

When Allison and I returned to our table, Blake stood and helped me with my chair. After I sat, he took my hand. Why did this man set my heart on fire?

At the same time our waiter brought out our food, a live band took the stage. They, too, were dressed classy. They reminded me of the bands from the 1940s my grandparents listened to. White sports coats, dark pants and shoes. Swing music? Jazz? I'd enjoy listening, but I hoped Blake didn't plan to dance.

After we were served, I peered across the table to see if Jim or Allison would offer a word of thanksgiving.

Blake squeezed my hand. "Let's pray." We all bowed our heads. "We thank you for bringing us together after several years to reinstate this family tradition. The family has changed, but Your faithfulness and provision have not. We are grateful, Lord. Amen."

Tears streamed down Allison's face. "Daddy. That was sweet."

"If I'd known I was going to make you cry, I would have asked Jim to pray." He gaped at me. "You too? What's wrong with you women?"

I glanced across the table at Allison. "A part of our job description. We like to laugh, cry, and go to the restroom in pairs. Coded into our brains."

I leaned closer to Blake but whispered loud enough for Allison and Jim to hear. "Could I have my hand back, so I can eat my dinner?" He released my hand. "Has anyone talked to Andy? Are he and Zoey coming for Christmas?" Zoey was Andy's girlfriend.

Allison frowned. "Dad's tried and so have I. Andy said they're not ready to make the trip yet."

Blake nodded. "I offered to buy their tickets, but I don't think Andy wants me to pay for them. He wants to be independent. The round-trip will cost them almost $1,000. They can't afford that kind of money, especially with a baby on the way."

After I finished the best steak I'd ever eaten, Blake asked if anyone wanted dessert. Allison and I declined. The guys ordered cheesecake—Jim peanut butter and Blake white chocolate.

When the waiter walked away, Blake nudged my arm. "Now's the time." He waggled his eyebrows.

My heart leapt. *Does he plan to kiss me right now? Here?* "Time?"

"Time to dance."

I panicked. Although the band played an array of genres, I didn't want to go out on the dance floor. Besides, this reminded me of Blake with Brandi. Not good memories.

He leaned close to my ear and whispered. "I anticipated a dance with you at the conference banquet. Things didn't go as planned." He stood and reached out his hand palm up. "Tonight, I don't want anything to interfere with our dance. I plan to sweep you off your feet my lovely lady."

I peered across the table, and Allison nodded. I stared up at Blake. "I don't know how to dance."

"I'll lead. You follow."

Allison and Jim encouraged me to go and have fun. Dancing wasn't fun when you hadn't swayed to music since your teen years. I'd be klutzy for sure. And with Allison and Jim nearby to watch me make a fool of myself, I dreaded what could happen.

I took Blake's offered hand, and he led me to the dance floor. I didn't know the song the band was playing, but the tune was soft and mellow. He placed my left hand on his right shoulder and took my right hand in his left. After he grinned, he put his right hand on the middle of my back and pulled me a little closer. *This is nice. Here on a date and I'm okay with that, for now.*

The song ended. Blake removed his hand from my back and put his index finger to his lips.

The band's leader said something about a special song for a special lady. He also mentioned the couple on the dance floor in blue. *We're in blue. What? What did he say?*

When the music restarted, Blake again placed his hand on my back and pulled me close. I gaped at him and tilted my head. His eyes glimmered. "This is my song to you."

His song to me? Blake sang along with the band's

lead singer. I glanced away. *Oh, my goodness. A love song.*

I gazed back into his blue eyes. Mine were met with admiration and love—unmistakable affection. "You're singing me a love song?"

He paused from his song to say one word. "Yes."

I guess I longingly looked at him because he whispered, "Not yet." But when the song ended, he dipped his head and leaned toward me. I put my fingers in front of his lips and forced a swallow. "Are you sure this time? This is a romantic moment to me, but I don't want to make the same mistake." I closed my eyes. His kiss was tender and sweet. My knees wobbled. I needed to sit.

He pulled back and caressed my cheek with his finger. "Was that a dream-worthy first kiss?"

I kept my eyes closed and waited for another. "I'm not sure. May I have a do-over?" I opened my eyes.

He chuckled. "Do-overs happen when the first time is messed up. Was my kiss bad?"

"If I say terrible, will I get another?" I smiled and winked.

"Do you think you can wait until I drive you home?"

"Promise?" I floated toward our table. "I'm going to need you to hold onto me. I'm feeling a little lightheaded."

"Are you okay?"

I stared at him. "Sparks are affecting my vision."

He grinned and kept his arm around my waist as we returned to our table.

Jim put his last bite of cheesecake into his mouth.

Blake patted him on the back before we sat.

"How's the cheesecake?" He eyed his piece on the other side the table. "Looks fantastic." He peered at me. "Would you like a bite?"

"You swept me off my feet, and all you can think about is your cheesecake?" I shook my head. "You're such a man."

Blake pulled out my chair and we sat.

I twisted toward him. "You have an amazing voice." *And lips.*

"You should hear him when he sings *and* plays." Allison beamed at her dad.

"Plays?"

Blake waved the comment off. "I play a little piano and the guitar. Nothing fancy."

"And the banjo." Jim peered at Blake's cheesecake. "That's my favorite."

I leaned closer to Blake. "You're full of surprises tonight. I realize how little I know you."

"You know all the important things."

Blake noticed Jim's continued stare and passed the rest of his cheesecake across the table. "Have at it, bud."

When we got ready to leave, Allison touched my arm and whispered. "You're glowing. He did sweep you off your feet, didn't he?"

"Unfortunately." I sighed.

She giggled. "Hang in there. You two make a great couple."

I shivered and rubbed my arms when we stepped outside. Blake wrapped his arm around my shoulders and pulled me close.

After we both settled into the car, I glanced at him. "Thank you for this evening."

"You mean our date?"

"Yes." I fiddled with the sequins on my dress. "Our date."

"So, we're dating now?"

I looked up at Blake and raised my eyebrows.

"And we're a couple, in a relationship, and no longer just special friends?"

"Is that what you meant by commit first?"

He shrugged. "What?" He stroked his stubbled chin. "Oh. You'll commit to be a couple because you want me to take you to another fancy place for dinner. I see how you are."

I gazed at him. His smile. What a transformation from a few months earlier.

Let him go. A voice pounded in my head. I startled and blinked. Stunned, I looked out the windshield and tried to compose myself. *Not the Lord.* A chill scurried down my spine. *Not real. Can't be.* I needed to respond, but what did Blake say? Commit to another dinner? Another date?

He took my hand. "Is everything okay?"

"Great. A beautiful evening." I continued to focus straight ahead. "I enjoyed meeting Jim. He and Allison make a cute couple." I tried to push aside what I thought I'd heard and was determined to enjoy the rest of my evening with Blake. After a chatty ride, we arrived at my place.

"Here we are. May I come in?" He squeezed my hand.

"Yes." *Or should I have said no?* I unlocked the door to my condo, and we strolled inside. "Would you like a cup of coffee or something else to drink?"

He shook his head and moved closer to me. His

eyes returned to my lips.

"Stop." I put my hand in front of his mouth.

He stepped back. "I thought you wanted—"

"I do. But could we go all the way back to the start of the song?"

"We don't have any music."

Thankful for a recent birthday gift, I cleared my throat. "Alexa." I asked her to play the same love song Blake sang to me—one of Jenny's favorites.

Blake held me in his arms—my hands draped around his neck. This dance was better than the last— no one watching us. During the instrumental part of the song he peered into my eyes and whispered, "I love you, K." His nickname for me.

Do I dare tell him how I feel? I searched his handsome face and again cupped his cheek in my hand. "And I love you."

68

Seven

Blake planned to arrive early Sunday morning. We wanted to grab a cup of coffee on our way to church. I glanced out my front window—eager to see him after spending most of the night awake remembering his arms around me, his song, and our kiss. I giggled. To find love a second time. And maybe, after several months of dating—marriage? I never planned on this. But there was still the issue of his lack of a relationship with God. I said a quick prayer that our pastor's message would touch Blake's heart. *If I do marry Blake, he must first commit himself to the Lord so we can love and serve Him together.*

I stepped out on my front porch when Blake pulled up to park. By the time I locked my front door, he was by my side. He'd shaved and looked great with or without the stubble. He escorted me to his car, and we drove to Starbucks. While we waited on our order, he was quiet and stared out the window. When I asked him if he was okay, he nodded. But something was off. He seemed distracted.

Let him go. That voice pounded in my head again.

Blake took my hand. "What's wrong? Your entire countenance changed."

I flushed and peeked at my watch. "Nothing. I'm good, but it's time to go."

I pressed my lips together. I was fine and in love, and Blake loved me. But God wanted me to let him go? *Why, Lord? Why now?*

During the worship service, I was able to push aside my thoughts and sing. This week I could hear Blake sing too. He must have hidden his gift last Sunday because I would have remembered his deep baritone voice.

Manuel walked to the platform.

I squeezed Blake's hand. "This will be good. He has a gift for teaching."

He spoke of hope, trusting in the Lord, and allowing God to take control. He shared stories from the Bible and personal experiences.

Blake squirmed and kept looking across the worship center. He crossed his legs and bounced his foot. A few minutes later, he released my hand, stood, and darted out into the hallway.

I grabbed my purse and Bible and followed him to the lobby. "What's wrong?" I reached for his arm.

He shook his head. "I got a text this morning that bothers me. The more I ponder it the more concerned I become."

I motioned to the café. "Let's go in there."

The café was housed inside the church bookstore. Windows aligned one side. That morning a few people lingered there. Two ladies occupied a table and a gentleman perused a book.

After we found a place in the corner next to a window, where we could talk uninterrupted, I said, "Are Allison and Andy okay?"

He took out his phone, opened his texts, and showed me two pictures. They were photos from Samson's. They weren't taken by Allison or Jim. The angle was wrong. Blake and I were on the dance floor. One photo was of us dancing and the other kissing.

"Who took these?" My hands shook.

"Lance Bailey." He placed his balled-up fist on the table. "The new VP in Legal."

"Legal? What did he say in the text?" I held my breath.

He glanced at his phone. "We need to talk on Monday. My office or yours?"

My heart raced. "What does this mean?"

"Not sure. But if Miranda's involved . . ." He reached for my hand.

~

Blake was terrible company the rest of the afternoon. He wanted to take me to lunch but said he wasn't hungry. I suggested we go to my place and have sandwiches. He agreed.

Inside the condo, Blake paced across my living room while I stood and watched him from my kitchen entrance.

"What's the worst-case scenario?" I asked.

"With Legal? Remember when I told you that Chad thought you should take the Admin Services Manager position when Bonnie Garfield retired?"

"I remember."

"He told me something Lance shared with the Executive Team last month while we were in New Mexico. There was a case of sexual harassment his last company was involved in."

My jaw dropped open. "Sexual harassment? That

doesn't apply to us."

"I know, and you know, but the company doesn't. Lance's employer took a big hit when this happened. The man involved was an executive. The woman was his administrative assistant." He stopped pacing and strode over to me. "She accused him of offering her a raise and promotion in return for favors. He claimed his innocence. She won the case. The company declared bankruptcy and shut down."

"I still don't see how that case relates to us." I bit my lower lip.

"Lance is working with Miranda on rewriting our harassment policy. Chad told me on Friday. Neither of us have seen their revisions yet. These pictures could fuel the fire."

"Sounds more than coincidental that you heard of these policy changes on Friday, and Lance decided to eat at the same restaurant we visited the following day." I kicked Roxie's catnip toy across the floor. "Of all the places in Nashville and Franklin we could have gone to for dinner and he shows up there?"

"I agree. Seems deliberate."

"I think we need to enjoy our afternoon and wait to see what happens tomorrow." I stepped into the kitchen and offered Blake a glass of sweet tea. "I can't believe BCH would point at us and think a sexual harassment case."

He faced me and placed his hands on my arms. "We need to protect the company in the future. Miranda has approached the Executive Team in the past and talked to them about updating our policy. And with the recent media coverage regarding women who have accused their employers of misconduct and abuse of power, now would be a perfect time for her to get her policy approved and use these pictures to make her case."

He wrapped his arms around me. "We'll figure something out." He kissed the side of my neck and whispered in my ear. "I'm not going to lose you."

If the voice in my head was the Lord, perhaps you will.

~

Blake stayed until 2:00 p.m. He appeared calmer when he left for home. We never did eat lunch. After he left, I fixed a chicken salad sandwich and sat at my kitchen table overlooking my tiny back yard. Lance and Miranda were revising our harassment policy. Lance showed up at Samson's and took pictures. More than odd. I didn't like this. What did Miranda want, and how did she convince Lance to join her side? I needed to get out of the house. I'd go crazy pondering this all afternoon and evening and decided to attend the children's Christmas program at church. But first, I needed to put up my artificial Christmas tree.

My fourth Christmas with a fake tree and without Sam. I still struggled with putting a tree up, but I knew Nicki expected one. In the past, Sam and I would drive to a tree farm and cut our own. Didn't seem like a tradition I could continue alone. I sat on my couch, stared at the box, and shook my head. I needed to get busy if I wanted to attend the program at church that evening.

I pulled my pre-lit tree out of the box and set it up in front of my living room window. Within two hours the tree was decorated. Nothing fancy but sufficient, and I still had time to change and drive to church.

Before the service, I searched for Manuel. I wanted to ask him to pray for Blake and me and this situation with Legal. I found him in the education wing.

"I've talked with Blake and told him that I'd be praying for you both," Manuel said.

"You talked with Blake? Today?"

"This situation with Legal has him bothered. Finding you after losing his wife. Now the threat of a policy interfering with the two of you being together. I'm glad he told you about Cheryl." He peered down the hallway at children getting rough with one another. "I'll be right back." He rushed down the hall.

Told me about Cheryl? Why does Manuel think Blake told me?

Manuel returned. "Difficult for Blake to believe God's forgiveness is for him since he hasn't been able to forgive himself. I've tried to reassure him that if she did die by her own hand, he's not to blame."

"Suicide?" I placed my hand on my chest and gasped.

Manuel turned white. "I thought you knew. Blake said he told you. Or did he say he planned to tell you?" He rubbed the back of his neck and glanced upward.

"You talk like you've spoken to Blake often. What's going on?"

"He didn't tell you we've been studying the book, *Second Chances*, together?"

"*Second Chances*? Not a word." I shook my head. "I knew he purchased the book after we met the author when we traveled to the healthcare conference last month. But I didn't know the two of you were discussing it together."

I stared at the floor and back at Manuel. "I need to

find Blake. He thinks if I know how Cheryl died, I'll blame him too." My voice caught. "I want to tell him that her death is not his fault. I won't hold that against him." I turned to leave and bumped into Manual's wife, Susie.

Manuel's deep voice rang loud and clear. "Let him go, Keedryn."

The sternness in his tone was more abrupt than the words I'd heard twice before. I stopped, clasped my hand over my mouth to stifle a cry, and trembled.

Susie wrapped her arms around me and held me close. She and Manuel led me to a classroom out of everyone's view and sat me down.

"No. Why? Why does God want me to let him go now?" I got down on my knees and bent over. My forehead rested on the carpet. "I asked Him over and over for four months to release me from my job at BCH. I believed He wanted me to stay. Why now?"

Manuel's tone was soft. "I don't know why." He sounded like he was behind me.

Either he or Susie held their hand on my back. "I believe the Lord directed me to speak those words to you. Blake loves you. But he needs to love God first. Right now, you're first."

I raised myself into a sitting position.

Manuel moved to face me and sat on the floor. "I sense maybe you, too, have given Blake first place in your heart."

My jaw slackened. "Me? God's in first place." I narrowed my eyes. "What are you trying to say?"

"Your eagerness to go to him without wanting to pray first."

"I haven't forgotten God. I would have prayed all

the way to Blake's house—wherever that is." I took a deep breath to calm myself. "I may have lost my focus this weekend." I stood to gather my thoughts. "I messed up everything." I placed the palm of my hand on my forehead and looked at Manuel. "Do you think the Lord said, 'Let him go' for a couple of weeks, months, years . . . or forever?"

Susie again wrapped her arms around me. Her embrace calmed me.

Manuel stood and rested his hand on my shoulder. "I don't know. God's not punishing you for losing your focus for a couple of days. He wants what's best for you." He cocked his head. "Blake may not be God's best."

I felt as though my heart sank to my toes.

"Or, maybe God wants to give Blake time without you, so he'll understand his need to return to the Lord. Blake needs to relearn to depend on God alone."

I began to pray aloud for God's hand to be upon Blake during his struggle with guilt over Cheryl's death and for his recommitment to the Lord. When I finished my prayer, Manuel took over. He asked the Lord to guide me in my relationship with Blake.

After we said amen, I hugged Manuel and Susie good-bye.

Blake, hurry back to God. Because . . . I love you.

Eight

After I put my purse in my desk drawer on Monday morning, I turned on my computer. What would today hold? A visit to Legal? A visit from Miranda? What did Chad think of this? Was I in the wrong to kiss Blake? Would he be reprimanded for inviting me to dinner? I shook my head. Why? Embarrassment and humiliation—that's what happens when you date someone you work with.

And I knew better.

Blake came out of his office, approached my desk, and spoke in a hushed tone. "HR and Legal are preparing a new policy that covers relationships between employees."

"Any details?"

"The meeting starts in fifteen minutes. The Executive Team must approve the policy. I doubt they'll allow me to vote. Chad told me that he'll move for a postponement, so we'll have more time to think this through. He believes a new policy is necessary, but not because of us. The board will have the final say."

Blake grabbed his coffee and trudged into the conference room. I couldn't concentrate on my work and prayed a useless prayer. If God wanted me to let

Blake go, why would this meeting turn out well for us? I hadn't experienced defeat like this since Sam died. Despair crept in.

Was Miranda in cahoots with any of those on the board? She apparently won over Lance easily enough.

The meeting seemed to take forever but didn't last as long as it felt. Chad, Lance, and Blake came out after an hour and proceeded to Blake's office without saying a word when they passed my desk. Blake was the last one in. He didn't slam the door—but close. Not a good sign.

I heard other voices in the conference room behind me but not well enough to know who remained in there. A minute later several board members and Miranda walked past our suite door. She strutted with her head held high and shoulders back. Not good.

I didn't know how to express to Blake how much I loved him, but I couldn't date him now—with or without a policy. And maybe never. I needed to follow the Lord's prompting and wait on His timing, as difficult as that was, but I didn't want Blake to blame God for this.

Several minutes passed before Blake poked his head out the door. "We'd like to talk with you."

When I entered, Lance motioned me to the empty chair across from Blake and led the conversation. "The new policy hasn't been finalized. But here's the gist." He cleared his throat. "It prohibits supervisors from having a relationship with or dating their subordinates but doesn't affect those in nonsupervisory positions unless both parties work in the same department. Anyone dating another employee must report this to HR. That's the policy in a nutshell."

Blake peered at me. "He has suggestions for those who may already be in a relationship or dating."

Lance directed all his attention to me. "The board is pushing for this policy. Your behavior Saturday evening caused them concern."

"My behavior?" I pressed my lips together. *How dare he.* All we did was dance and kiss. Once.

Lance motioned toward Blake. "He can explain later."

"He's referring to both of us. Not only you," Blake said.

"If employees within the same department want to date, or supervisors want to date those who report to them, the following options are available. One can resign. Or one can transfer to another department if an opening exists that meets their qualifications." Lance glanced at Blake and back to me. "However, in your case, nothing is available."

I frowned. "Has Bonnie Garfield's position been filled?"

"We hired an external applicant."

I leaned toward him to suggest an idea. A good one. "Any possibility of a job switch? I could take an administrative assistant position. The assistant from that department could become Blake's executive assistant." I looked at Blake for support. "I'd take a cut in pay but wouldn't need to resign."

"Great idea. Lance?" Blake sounded hopeful.

"That's a possibility we haven't discussed." He stroked his chin. "If that doesn't work out, will you resign?"

I pulled at my collar. Blake's office never felt this warm before. "You're making the assumption I will."

Lance grinned. "That's your only option. You or Blake." He pointed to Blake and shook his head. "I can't believe you'd expect him to give up *his* position." He smirked.

Blake's eyes narrowed. "We'd like to discuss this alone." He stood, strode to his door, and opened it.

Lance nodded. "Let me know what you decide. The policy is scheduled to go into effect in two weeks."

His smug expression made me want to slap him across the face. I steadied my breathing and kept my mouth shut.

Lance stood and made his way to the door. He stopped and again focused his attention on me. "This is a zero-tolerance policy. You'll both be terminated if you continue to date or behave in an inappropriate manner."

Blake's face was red, and his fists were clenched at his sides.

Lance bolted out the door.

Up to this time, Chad remained quiet. He looked at me. "You've been a miracle worker with Blake these past few months. Now this. All I can say is, if God wants you two to be together, this policy won't stop Him." He stood. "Due to recent media coverage, this policy was inevitable. I'll leave you alone to talk this over." He closed the door on his way out.

Blake sat next to me and crossed his arms. "You seem calm in light of this situation. Do you understand what this means?"

"Of course, I understand." I peered at the table. "I don't want to resign. I enjoy my job and need the income." I relaxed my shoulders. "I should have taken Bonnie's position."

He lifted my chin. "Let's consider option three."

I tilted my head and gazed into his gorgeous eyes. "There wasn't an option three." I scrunched up my face.

He beamed. "We can get secretly engaged now and married in two weeks before the policy takes effect."

I chuckled, and his smile faded. "You were serious? I'm sorry. I thought you . . ." I placed my elbow on the table, my hand on my forehead, and closed my eyes—*Lord, help me.* I lifted my eyes back to his. "I love you. But I'm not ready to make a commitment under pressure. And getting married in two weeks would be a lot of pressure. Besides, I'd still need to resign. Family members can't work together either if one supervises the other."

His mouth twisted. "You'd need to resign. But you wouldn't need the job. I'd take care of you. You wouldn't need to search for another position unless you wanted to."

I glanced toward the ceiling and back to Blake.

He shook his head. "I know that wasn't a romantic proposal, but . . ." He slumped back into his chair.

I touched his arm. "Accepting your proposal and becoming engaged is a commitment. One I can't make this soon. I think our only option now is number four."

He rubbed his chin and spoke slowly. "And what is option four?"

"Maybe the policy won't be approved by the board. I think we should wait it out. Not see each other except here in the office. Give this a chance to go away."

"That's your plan? I'm not fond of option four. Makes no sense." He shrugged. "Let's get together tonight and discuss this further." He took my hand in his and gazed into my eyes. "I want to spend every free minute with you these next two weeks. Dinner at the finest restaurants, dancing, singing. Maybe I can change your mind about making a commitment."

I squeezed his hand. "I can't think of anything I'd enjoy more than to spend time with you. But doing so will make this harder for both of us."

He wrinkled his forehead and leaned back in the chair. "You're giving up? On us? I don't understand."

I couldn't hold back the tears. "I love you. But I can't marry you," I whispered. "I'm sorry." I darted from his office and zipped down the hall.

My heart not only broke for me but for Blake.

~

By the time I arrived home that evening I was exhausted. I needed a diversion. Nicki would work fine, but Jenny and Carl had plans. I came up with an idea at Samson's when we discussed Andy and Zoey. Now was the time to see it through.

Maybe Andy wouldn't allow Blake to help him with airline tickets, but if he thought they could surprise his dad and Allison for Christmas, maybe he'd allow me to pay. I wanted to give them all a gift. What did you give a rich guy like Blake and his family? This would be perfect.

I called Andy's number. While we chatted, he told me that he and Zoey were doing well, and their baby was due in mid-March.

"I'd like to surprise Blake and Allison with a visit from you and Zoey. I'll purchase your tickets if you'll agree to arrive on Christmas Day, because fares are a little cheaper. What do you think?"

Andy laughed. "We should say no. But that will be dope to see Dad's and Allison's faces when they answer the door."

We made plans for them to arrive at 4:30 p.m. on December 25 and leave the following Sunday at 2:30 p.m. They would have five days to spend with family. I got their ID information for the tickets and reminded them to keep this a surprise.

84

Nine

The remainder of our week didn't go well. Anyone who came into our office must have thought we didn't like each other much. We barely spoke. I'd be frustrated, too, if I were Blake. He proposed, and I laughed. He wanted to spend every free minute with me during the two weeks before the policy took effect, and I brushed him off. He had every right to be upset with me.

When he asked me if I'd given up on us, I felt like my heart had been ripped from my chest. I didn't know what to do except continue to pray.

On Friday afternoon, Chad caught me in the hallway. "What's going on with you two? Blake's given up fighting this."

I kept my voice low. "Is there a way to fight it?" I waved my hands. "This is some vendetta of Miranda's."

He glanced down the hall. "Come to my office."

In his office, a mirror image of Blake's, Chad motioned to a chair at his conference table. We both took a seat.

"Why did you say Miranda has a vendetta?" Chad asked.

"She tampered with Blake's presentation to make

me appear incompetent."

Chad held up his hand to stop me. "An assumption on your part. To my knowledge, that has not been proven. Stick with the facts."

I took a deep breath and exhaled slowly. "When she offered me Bonnie's job, she insisted I move downstairs. She got huffy with Blake when he suggested I stay upstairs, and we share an assistant. She also tried to pressure me to offer the new assistant position to Alicia because she's Walt's niece. When I told Miranda that Alicia wasn't qualified, she said, 'I'd be careful if I were you.' Sounded like a threat to me."

Chad nodded. "Go on."

"I didn't want the position after that. She said she'd talk to Beth regarding Bonnie's position but never did." I paused to think about what I wanted to say next. "This policy is her crusade to get rid of me. She's jealous. Doesn't want me near Blake. Well I'm not going anywhere." I crossed my arms.

Chad sat back in his chair and allowed me to vent. "I'm happy you plan to stay." He paused. "But sounds to me that you're the reason Blake stopped fighting the policy. Why? So you can prove your point to Miranda?"

"I don't want to prove a point to anyone." I cocked my head. "I'm not ready to resign. I need my job. More importantly, I enjoy it."

He leaned closer and peered into my eyes. "Your job is more important than Blake. Is that what you said?"

I'd not seen this side of Chad before. Devil's advocate didn't become him. "No. You're twisting what I said." I closed my eyes for a moment to collect my thoughts. "I'm crushed by all of this. Why should a policy dictate people's lives?"

Chad inhaled a deep breath and blew out slowly. "Policies inform and guide. They protect employees and employers alike. This one is touchy because of the timing." He glanced across his office. "If we'd enforced a dating policy six months ago, like we should have, we wouldn't be having this conversation. You'd both have known not to get involved, or you would have taken Bonnie's position without hesitation."

"There should be a clause that states couples currently dating are exempt. Could that be passed?"

"The board of directors are concerned in relation to current happenings in the media. Although, if we didn't have the pictures, perhaps we could fight for an exemption."

"The photos?"

"Blake told me that he showed those to you."

"Yes, I've seen them. I have questions as to how Lance ended up at the same restaurant as us." I drummed my fingers on the table. "I didn't go to Samson's with Blake. Allison and her husband picked me up. I think Lance was staked out at my place and followed me there. I'll bet I could verify that with my neighbors. Someone saw something." I grimaced. "I'm convinced he and Miranda are partners in crime."

"I find this situation odd too." Chad softened his tone. "One day before your date, Miranda insists on changes to our current harassment policy. Two days after, there's a push for an entirely new policy. Sounds personal." Chad leaned back in his chair. "The board scrutinized one more thing."

"In addition to the photos?"

"Yes. Rumors. But I don't believe them."

"With Beth out this week and Tauni super busy, I haven't heard anything specific. I have noticed staff in the lobby when I walk by. Whispers and nods." I stared at the closed door. "Have you heard from Beth? She told me earlier in the week that her husband was ill. Is he doing better?"

"Yes. She should be back on Monday. She probably doesn't know about the rumors."

"I'll call her and check on her husband. See if she needs anything." I shook my head. "Funny. Blake's a different person than when I first became his assistant." I peered at Chad. "You've gotten the old Blake back. Why would someone try to undermine us and destroy that?"

"You do care for him, don't you?"

"I love Blake." I needed to stop and steady my voice. "But this doesn't appear good for us."

I slumped back into my chair. I cared about Blake much more than my job. But if I resigned, I'd lose both. *How do I explain "Let him go" without turning Blake further away from the Lord?*

"Hopefully, that's enough for him to hang onto. We have another week to come up with something. Don't give up yet." Chad stood. "I'll ask the board if we can exempt those who are already in relationships, but I don't expect them to comply."

I thanked Chad for his time and left. On the way to my desk, I saw Tauni and Wes coming down the hallway. "Looking for me?"

Tauni nodded. "Can we use the conference room?" She grabbed my arm while we walked and apologized for canceling our lunch on Wednesday. "I worked through lunch to get caught up."

I assured her that I understood.

Inside the conference room, Wes said, "As your friends, we want to tell you what we've heard throughout the office."

I motioned them to a chair. Wes moved to the far side of the table, and Tauni and I sat next to one another. "Please do. I know rumors have surfaced, but I haven't heard any."

"The word is that you and Blake got drunk together Saturday evening. Pictures prove the two of you behaved unprofessionally. You plan to resign because of a new policy."

"And what do you, my friends, say?"

"You don't drink. Therefore, none of it happened." Tauni tapped her fist on the table.

"I love you, Tauni." I smiled and touched her hand. "You two are special to me. Neither of us drank. We did dance, and Blake kissed me after the dance. Those are the two pictures that were taken. Allison and Jim were with us. We were double dating. Blake took me home but didn't stay long."

Wes squirmed. "Is there a possibility you may move in with him?"

My mouth fell open. "No way. Is that one of the rumors? I think you know me better than that. If I move in with anyone, there will be a ring on my finger and a marriage license in my hand."

Moving in with Blake? I had a good idea of who started that. But how would we put a stop to them?

Tauni leaned toward me. "What are you going to do? Will you resign?"

"Right now, I believe the Lord wants me to wait it

out."

Wes stood and began to pace. "Tauni and I have discussed this and prayed. We've come up with a plan to get people to stop their talk about you and Blake in a negative way."

Tauni opened her eyes wide. "If you appeared to be dating someone else, people would stop. They'd think you and Blake are no longer a couple."

"A good idea. But I'm still not into the dating thing." I felt nauseated. "Look where one date with Blake got me. In the middle of a huge mess."

Wes stopped pacing and gazed at me. "And that's why I'm offering my services as a friend. No strings attached."

"Sweet, but I can't ask you to do that." I let out a long breath.

"You didn't. I volunteered. That's what friends do. We can start Monday for lunch."

I needed to think. I rubbed my temples. "Might work." I glanced at Wes. "No. Won't work." This could get messy too. Wes told me two weeks before that he wanted to date me.

Wes frowned. "I'm trying to help. How successful will you be dispelling rumors by waiting it out? You need an ally. Take it or leave it—up to you."

"Okay. No. Wait. Are you sure?" A crazy idea. I didn't want to hurt him again.

"I need to get back to my desk before my boss notices I'm gone. I'll talk to you later." Wes took a couple of steps toward the door.

I wrung my hands together. "Let's try."

Blake stepped into the conference room. "I hate to break this up, but Keedryn, I have things I need you to do before we call it quits today."

"I'll be right there."

I peered at Tauni and Wes. "Thanks for having my back. I appreciate you both."

With my stomach in knots, I zipped into Blake's office and asked him what he needed me to do.

He got up from his desk, closed his office door, and plodded to the round table. "Sit here at the table with me. I need to tell you something."

I sat and waited patiently for him to speak.

He cleared his throat. "If you can't marry me and want to continue to work here, we need to date other people. The rumors have gotten worse. I don't want to subject you to what people have said."

"About us? I heard the rumors from Wes and Tauni. They came as friends to tell me."

"Drinking and moving in together?"

"Blake. We know the truth. Such a beautiful evening." I bit my lip. "No one can destroy that for me. No matter what happens between us, Saturday evening will be one of the best memories of my life. An experience I'll forever cherish."

He glanced at the table, stood, and sat again.

What now?

"I plan to go on a couple of dates with Eliza Walker. She's available and won't be a threat to you in any way."

I closed my eyes for a moment and willed the tears to stay away. "Eliza? Will I be able to meet her?"

"She'll be here on Monday to meet me for lunch. I'll ask her to come up, so I can introduce you."

He rose and strode to his desk before I could respond. I stood. "I'm having lunch, too, on Monday.

Wes and I also plan to date. You don't have to be concerned about him, either. He thought our dating might help quench the rumors too. He came up with the idea."

"I'll bet he did." Blake sounded annoyed. "You plan to spend time with someone you admire and enjoy a friendship with. I'm pretending to date someone I can barely stand to be near and have nothing in common with."

"I plan to go out with someone who respects me and will not try to take advantage of my situation." I raised my voice. "You're spending time with someone who has the reputation of a floozy."

His mouth twisted. "I think you outdid me. I don't have a good comeback. She is a floozy." He stepped to the front of his desk and faced me. "What are we doing? Say the word. I'll resign, and we can continue our relationship. You can take as long as you need to decide if you want to marry me."

I covered my mouth. After a moment, I pulled my hand away. "Blake. I want to say yes. I want to marry you and spend the rest of my life with you." I looked at the file folders on his desk. "But it's not about me. I need to wait on the Lord. He hasn't told me yes, yet." I peered at Blake and whispered. "I'm praying He will."

"We're waiting on God?" He stared at me with wide eyes and raised eyebrows.

I nodded.

He leaned back against his desk. "I doubt He thinks I'm good enough for you. I was a lousy husband to Cheryl. He knows you deserve better than me."

I touched his arm. "What are you doing tonight?"

We arranged to meet at a public library at 7:00

p.m. We'd be able to talk quietly but be public enough if we were followed. We didn't want to be accused of sneaking around. I suggested a rule—no touching. We couldn't give anyone reason to gossip.

On my drive home I called Manuel and asked if he'd spoken to Blake since Sunday evening. I told Manuel that Blake and I would be meeting later that evening, and I wanted to reassure him he'd been a good husband to Cheryl. Manuel said he would call or arrange to meet Blake before 7:00 and break the news to him.

When Blake and I met at the library, we found a table in the corner near a small decorated Christmas tree and sat across from one another. Not where I longed to be. I would have preferred to sit next to him with his arm around me and my head on his shoulder. But right now, he needed hope and encouragement. And I needed the Lord to move in his life, so I didn't have to worry about Eliza sinking her claws into my man.

I said a quick prayer for the Holy Spirit to guide me. I wanted to respond to Blake's comment regarding God not thinking he was good enough for me and reassure him he wasn't a lousy husband to Cheryl. "I believe you were an excellent husband. You loved Cheryl and modeled for your children a loving relationship. Look at the way Allison treats Jim. The way Andy treats Zoey. You did that Blake. You and Cheryl together."

After saying that he and Manuel had talked, Blake hung his head. "I wasn't able to keep Cheryl alive or my family together. I blame myself for her death. We fought. She was depressed, and I made things worse.

She left upset. Does that sound like a good husband to you?"

Despite our agreement I took his hand in mine. "I'm sorry you endured that kind of pain and heartache. Her depression must have been torment for you. You wanting to help her, and she not willing to receive your help. That's what the argument was about, wasn't it? The one Andy overheard."

"I arranged to take her to a hospital where they specialized in suicidal care. I couldn't help her. She wouldn't let me." He lifted his face—his eyes dull and moist. "I failed her. I failed Allison, Andy, and God."

I squeezed his hand. "Maybe this isn't the best place for us to be. Do you want to go to my place?"

"Do you think we could talk at your daughter's? Carl mentioned they have a bonus room upstairs. That should be private."

I called Jenny, and she said we could use the room. Nicki would soon be in bed, and we'd have our privacy. Blake followed me there, and we were warmly greeted by Carl and Jenny along with Lucy, their beagle.

On our way to the stairs, I noticed their tree in the living room. "The top part of your Christmas tree is beautiful. Did Nicki help with the bottom?"

"Could you tell by her handmade ornaments? She did a better job this year than last." Jenny chuckled. "Lucy wanted to help too. She ran through, knocked the tinsel off, and Nicki put it back on."

We climbed the stairs, and I motioned for Blake to sit on the sofa. I sat across from him in a chair. "I believe you were a wonderful husband. You've carried guilt and shame that you weren't meant to carry." He looked everywhere but at me. "Cheryl was ill. Andy told me when we were in Albuquerque that you spent extra time at home. I believe you did that to watch over her because you didn't want to leave her alone. You showed her unconditional love."

Blake glanced my way. "Not enough."

I tilted my head. "Jesus took your shame and guilt to the cross with Him—not yours to carry. Let it go."

That's what this was about. He needed to let it go like I needed to let him go. For Blake to be totally free from this guilt, he must let it go and trust God.

I leaned toward him. "Do you love me?"

"I love you with everything in me. You know I do."

"Then let Cheryl go."

"Cheryl? You think I'm holding onto her?"

"I think you're holding onto the sad memories of her and not the good. Let go of the pain and suffering and remember the love and laughter."

He gave a slow nod.

"One more thing." I spoke in a soothing tone. "You told me, 'I love you with everything in me.' As wonderful as that is for me to hear, the Lord desires that same kind of devotion from you."

Ten

I spent the weekend like I'd spent most of my week—more time in God's Word and prayer. To do this, I skipped a few meals. Several times I pleaded with the Lord for answers and direction. Finally, I surrendered to His will. The answer, I believed, lay in Blake doing what I'd shared with him on Friday evening. When he could honestly say he loved the Lord with everything in him, the Lord would welcome our relationship and give us the desires of our heart. My desire now was to marry Blake.

I struggled with him and Eliza spending time together. Tauni, during her wayward time, was tame compared to what I'd heard regarding Eliza. Blake knew I was waiting on God and why I couldn't say yes to his proposal. I hoped he would wait for God's timing and not give up on me.

~

Normally I leave for work at 7:30 a.m. to arrive a little before 8:00, my scheduled start time. However, on Monday morning at 7:00, my doorbell rang. To receive visitors at home that early in the morning was rare. I turned on my porch light and peeked out my front window. Why was Allison's husband, Jim, here? My heart sank. Had something happened to Allison or Blake?

I opened the door. "Is everything okay?"

He assured me everyone was fine. "Blake asked me to deliver this to you. He didn't think it would be wise to give it to you at the office."

Jim held a single, lovely rose wrapped in a paper towel to keep it moist. He gave it to me along with a handwritten note from Blake. I thanked him, and he left.

This flower was a salmon color. The outer petals displayed a darker pinkish tint and the inner a softer orange. I remembered from our time in Albuquerque this color meant excitement. Exquisite. The note read: "You've become my one-and-only."

He melts my heart. This gift brought me hope that Blake would wait for me.

When I arrived at the office, I knew the top item on my agenda for the week—make sure everything was ready for the executive team's holiday party. Saturday was the big day. Beth was back in the office, and Tauni stepped in to take most of Alicia's planning responsibilities. We met in the conference room to review all arrangements.

I took a seat at the table across from Beth and Tauni and asked Beth about her husband's health.

"He's much better. He had bronchitis and was in a lot of pain with all the coughing. Thanks again for your phone call." She smiled. "Is Alicia still planning to take care of the bar?"

"I'll check with her." Tauni made a note on her pad. "That's the only thing on her list. I'll ask Mitch to help if she hasn't followed through."

"And I have everything ready to pick up on schedule," Beth said.

I marked off the items on my checklist. "Great. Jenny and I verified with our church cooks, and all is well there too."

I was interrupted by an intercom page to call the front desk. Walt was on the phone and upset. "Put him through. We're in a meeting now planning the holiday party." I placed the call on speaker and greeted Walt.

"Where's Blake?" Short and snippy. "He didn't answer his phone."

"He's out this morning. I believe he plans to be back by—"

"I didn't ask when he'd be back. Where is he?"

Tauni glared at the phone and I rolled my eyes. Walt was never overly pleasant, but not usually this gruff either. "I wasn't trying to avoid your question. Blake's at—"

"Doesn't matter. We need to change the holiday party."

I glanced at Tauni and Beth. Four large eyes stared back at me. "Change it?"

"That's what I said, Ms. Reynolds. Is something wrong with your hearing?"

"No. Sir. Why do we need to change the party?" I pressed my lips together. I was not fond of this man.

"Let's plan for the following weekend."

You must be kidding. "Three days before Christmas?"

"Is that a problem?"

"Not for me, but people might already have plans for that weekend." I shifted focus. "Why do we need to change the party?"

"I have to fly to Florida to visit my wife. She's there with her mother who's taken a turn for the worse. May not survive this time. I can't have the party at my place. I won't be there."

"I'm sorry about your mother-in-law. Maybe Blake can host the party at his place." I nodded at Beth and Tauni and brought my hands together. "You said he has a big house too. Do you think that'll work?"

"Are you telling me you still haven't been in his house?"

"Correct. I've never even seen a picture of his place."

"Interesting." He paused. "I heard you moved in with him." He sounded like he didn't believe me.

I placed my elbow on the table and rubbed my forehead. "A rumor, Walt. A disgusting rumor." I shook my head. *Lies. Lance? Miranda? Why?*

"This will be the first holiday party I've missed. I'd rather postpone."

"I'm sure you'll be missed too." *Forgive me, Lord. I don't believe that at all.* I looked up and saw Tauni and Beth holding their hands over their mouths and nearly laughed myself.

"Go ahead and see if the executive team can use Blake's place. He won't like the idea of the bar. We usually have people who can't drive home, and he'll have to find them a ride or put them up for the night. But he'll make a lot of enemies if he doesn't have one. And he can't afford to offend anyone with this indiscretion hanging over his head."

I jerked my head up.

Beth waved her hands and mouthed, "Keep your cool. Don't anger the Chairman."

I took a deep, long breath. "I'll ask him."

I hung up and peered at Tauni and Beth. "Can you believe that man? Blake's indiscretion? Since when is a little kiss an indiscretion? We didn't do anything wrong."

Tauni and Beth stood, walked to my side of the table, leaned over, and embraced me in a group hug. They prayed a sweet prayer over me too. Afterward, I told them that when I cleared the move in the location for the party with Blake, we would notify every one of the change. We ended our meeting thankful things were coming together well.

Blake arrived at 8:45 and appeared to be in a good mood.

"I love the rose," I whispered. "The color is like an Albuquerque sunrise."

"My gardener grows them in a greenhouse year-round."

"Beautiful," I said and told him about the call from Walt.

"Where can you have the party on such short notice?"

I winced. "I hoped since we'll be there preparing food, we could use your place. I doubt I can find another location this close to the date."

Blake cited the alcohol, clean-up, and not being able to leave early as reasons against being the party's host. When I suggested we cancel everything, he agreed to have the bash at his place.

Eliza arrived to meet Blake for lunch at 11:30. When Blake introduced us, she acted like meeting me was an inconvenience. She grasped his arm and clung to him on their way out the door.

I met Wes in the lobby a few minutes later. Our lunch wasn't as comfortable as those in the past—more than awkward. I kept my conversation upbeat and didn't get personal concerning anything. I needed to be careful not to give him any false hope where the two of us were concerned.

~

By Friday, my confidence soared. The party would be a success. I would have been doomed if not for Beth and Tauni and their willingness to meet and work through the details during lunch every day except Monday. We made a good team and managed to add in fun and laughter to our workload.

Blake appeared stressed during the week. A couple of times, I saw him pace while on his cell. On Friday afternoon, I managed to find a few minutes to talk with him in his office.

When I entered, I sat across from him at his desk. His elbow rested on top of papers with his palm covering his eyes. "Headache? I have Advil."

He jerked his head up. "No. I was trying to hide. I see it didn't work."

"Everything will work out." I straightened papers on his desk. "What's your biggest struggle right now?"

"Eliza. She calls me every day. She stops by the house. She thinks we're a couple now."

"After one lunch?"

He spoke in a grumpy tone. "I'm concerned about tomorrow night. She's now the hostess at my house. Who knows what ideas that will put into her head? Would have been better to have this at Walt's."

~

Jenny came by Saturday morning at 9:00 to pick

me up. When she entered my foyer, she acted like a young princess being invited to the king's palace to meet her prince. "Remember how I loved to watch the Cinderella movies? Dad would sit with me and tell me I would always be his princess." She rubbed her eyes. "He'd take me in his arms, let me stand on his feet, and dance with me all over the living room." She imitated their dance steps.

"I remember it well."

"Don't be surprised if I take off spinning and twirling at Blake's house. I'm expecting the night to be something out of a fairy tale."

I wasn't as excited as she was to see Blake's house or to be further involved with this party. The thought made me nervous. First, I didn't want to run into Eliza again. My goal was to get out of Blake's house before that woman arrived. Knowing she put pressure on Blake, her need for them to be a couple, made my stomach curl.

Second, though I was confident we had everything well planned for the party, if something went wrong, I'd take the blame. That was a lot of pressure. I awaited 5:00 p.m. when I could leave.

Beth and Allison were at Blake's when we arrived. Tauni came shortly after. Wes sent a text and said he was bringing breakfast snacks.

I stood in awe in the foyer and gaped. Blake's entryway was more elegant than Walt's. The stairway in front of me branched off to the right and left to a balcony overlooking the mammoth foyer. Ornate white pillars loomed along both sides of the staircase. A sitting room to the right of the front door and an open great room behind the stairway were richly decorated in the finest upholstery and window coverings. The rooms were aglow with morning light. Windows galore—stunning.

Allison led us to the kitchen by way of a short hallway to the left and past a formal dining room. Four ovens and a pantry the size of my kitchen stood to the left. The kitchen's dining area sat to the right. Behind the seating area, a staircase led to the second floor and a door led to the backyard. The granite countertops looked like a contemporary painting. The array of colors swirled around in an elaborate design of bluish gray, deep green, light tan, and rust. God's handiwork.

"I could fit ten of my kitchens in here. This is enormous and beautiful. This granite is amazing."

"You could be mistress of all this," Allison whispered.

"Have you heard what's going on with us?"

"Dad assures me the situation's temporary."

I stared at the floor. "I hope you're right."

Allison linked her elbow with mine. "I'm going to do my best to keep her away from him as much as possible."

"Are we talking about Eliza or Miranda?"

"Both." She kept her voice low. "But Eliza is your biggest threat. I never understood why Mom chose her as a friend. She's evil."

Allison confirmed what Beth had told me weeks earlier.

I scanned the kitchen. "Where's your dad this morning?"

"He's running errands. He likes to stay busy on the weekends. He said he'd go by and visit Tim this afternoon too."

"I look forward to meeting your son."

"That would be great." Allison scurried away and assisted one of the church ladies find the utensils she needed.

Wes arrived with pastries, breakfast biscuits, and muffins. I passed. He asked me if we were on for lunch again on Monday, and I confirmed.

The team worked all morning, moved furniture, set up tables and chairs, and decorated in festive colors of red and green. Fortunately, Allison and Jim came over the day before and put up four Christmas trees with all the trimmings.

Before lunch we prepared our dessert trays. Unlike me, Allison and Jenny had a flair for decorating food trays. Preparations were coming together well. I thanked each person for the help and time they'd put into making this a special evening.

I peeked at my watch—almost 4:30. We were on schedule, and I was ready to relax. Jenny and I planned to leave soon to go home, change, and take Nicki to the Grand Ole Opry. A great place to take my mind off Eliza, Blake, and the party.

I strolled over to the dining area of the kitchen to sit and rest. Before I pulled out a chair, I saw Blake.

He came down the set of stairs at the far edge of the kitchen. He was dressed in a black sports coat with a light gray, open collared shirt which complimented his salt and pepper gray hair. His eyes twinkled when he saw me. "Looks like things are coming along well." He stepped closer. "How are you doing?" he whispered.

"I'm tired—been a long day." I wrinkled my nose.

"I'm concerned about you."

"Because I'm tired? I'm fine."

"That and you've lost weight these past couple of weeks." He eyed me, making me uncomfortable. "When was the last time you saw a doctor?"

"Don't worry." I yawned and patted my cheeks. "Jenny and I need to leave by 5:00. I'll sit and rest at the Opry. I hope everyone here has a good time."

"Before you go, I want to tell you something important." He got close to my ear. "I still love you with everything in me."

"I love you too," I whispered.

I felt spiritually stronger since I'd increased my praying and Bible reading, and I sensed the Lord's presence more than ever. But my emotions were raw. I worked hard to keep tears at bay.

Jenny hurried over to us. "I heard from Carl. Nicki's running a fever. She took a nap and woke up feeling sick with a temperature of 101 degrees." Jenny wrung her hands. "We can't go to the Opry tonight. Nicki's back in bed." Jenny looked at me. "We can stay and help."

Concern etched Blake's face. "You should both go home."

Jenny smiled at Blake. "Carl's taking care of her. We'll celebrate tomorrow. She'll miss out on Scotty though. She'll be heartbroken."

Blake shook his head. "Nope. Won't let my little Nicki be heartbroken." The corner of his eyes crinkled. "I'll take care of this."

Eleven

At 5:00 p.m., the doorbell announced the arrival of the first guest, or should I say, hostess. I was in the great room helping with food layout. Earlier, we placed the buffet tables along the left wall of the great room close to the kitchen. The wide staircase blocked a lot of the foyer, but from where I stood near the tables, I couldn't miss her entrance. Although, I wish I had.

Eliza Walker entered with pizazz. She looked glamorous wearing a sparkling red dress that fell well below her knees. Some of that fabric would have been better used at her neckline. Her long, wavy, black hair curled over her shoulders. Her perfectly tanned skin and red lipstick that matched her dress added to her exquisite beauty.

Her exuberance in greeting Blake nearly knocked him over. She wasted no time in planting a big kiss on his lips.

"Smart man." I muttered under my breath. "Don't act like you enjoy that with me nearby."

Allison stood next to me and snarled. "Your fairy tale now has a wicked witch."

"I'm afraid we're in for a long night." I sighed and

plodded back to the kitchen.

There, Jenny took me aside. "Do you want me to go home to grab a different outfit? I could go by your place, too, and pick something up for you. We'll be confined to the kitchen in our jeans." Her eyes darted around the room. "The others brought a change of clothes."

"No problem for me to stay in the kitchen. I don't want to see what's going on out there. I've seen enough." I padded to a chair. "I need to sit for a few minutes, though. I'm tired."

"Let me get you something to eat. No arguing." She pointed her finger at me like she was the mom. "You need strength to get through tonight."

"I'm good. I don't need anything."

Jenny put her hands on her hips. "I hope Blake realizes soon what you're doing for him. Denying yourself to pray for God to move in his heart and change him."

"No, Jenny." I chuckled at her dramatic pose. "Prayers for him to let go of his past and find love, acceptance, and forgiveness in the Lord."

Allison strolled over to the table where we talked and placed a plate of smoked brisket, chicken, and sausage in front of me with all the trimmings. The aroma stirred up pangs of hunger.

My eyes met hers. "Nothing for me, thank you."

She mimicked Jenny's pose. "Two against one. Eat or I'll drive you home."

I picked up the fork and dove into the brisket. Jenny and Allison stood on each side of me. "Could I eat in private, please? Either that or sit." I looked up and frowned. "You two make me nervous."

Allison sat next to me while Jenny talked to Wes. "Dad's a blessed man to have you in his life. Thanks for loving him so much."

I placed my index finger in front of my lips. "Shh. We don't want anyone to hear."

Guests arrived and the increased noise level in the great room floated down the hallway to the kitchen. The serving team worked well together keeping the food replenished. Desserts were laid out, and the servers reported that everyone seemed to enjoy the meal. With Jenny and me relegated to the kitchen, we washed dishes and kept the area tidy.

The band played softly during the meal. When they turned up their amplifiers, Tauni danced her way into the kitchen. "They've got their party on out there." She peered at me. "You should peek in. They're letting all inhibitions go on the dance floor."

"I'm good. That's all I need to know." My interest in the party left me at 5:00. I kept reliving Eliza's enthusiasm and forwardness when she greeted Blake.

I prepared two fresh pots of coffee and turned to see who could take them into the great room.

Wes stood nearby. "I'll take those. When I get back, would you like me to take you home? I'll be happy to drive you."

I shook my head and thanked him. "I'll let you know if I change my mind."

Five minutes later, at 8:00, Miranda came into the kitchen and waltzed over to where I washed dishes. "We need a couple of dessert trays and fresh coffee. Immediately."

"Wes took in the coffee." I scanned the kitchen to see if he was nearby. "I'll ask Beth to bring in more dessert trays."

"I want you to bring them in. Now." Her snippy tone made me uneasy. Hadn't she caused enough pain? Now she wanted to humiliate me.

"But I'm not dressed to go in there. I didn't plan to stay this late or bring extra clothes."

"You're fine." She batted her hand at me. "Bring the trays."

Not fine. She's up to something. "I was told we have a protocol for serving at company functions. As HR Director, you want me to go against normal procedure and take in dessert trays dressed inappropriately?"

Miranda got in my face. "As HR Director, that is exactly what I want you to do." She whirled and sashayed in the direction of the party.

I didn't want her to get out the door until she answered all my questions. I spoke in a louder tone than normal. "Explain to me which procedures I must follow and which I may disregard."

She stopped and spun toward me. "You cannot disregard any of them." Her eyes flashed. "But I have the authority in my position to allow a waiver this one time." She turned and slithered out the kitchen door.

Those who'd overheard stared at me.

"I guess I better get in there." I gazed upward and down again and grabbed the trays. Didn't take long for me to understand why she insisted I bring the dessert. The band was playing the love song Blake sang to me at Samson's. Miranda must have requested it. I assumed she wanted me in the great room to see Blake and Eliza on the dance floor together.

But when I saw people staring at me, I looked

down—dishwater covered the front of my blouse. Either that or they hoped to witness the despair of a jilted woman. I turned my back to the dance floor and focused my eyes on the dessert table. I placed the two trays next to the fresh coffee and tidied up the napkins, spoons, and sugar packets so as not to appear in a hurry to run off. But I wanted to run. Hard to stay and have coworkers and board members gawk and watch my every move.

"They make a lovely couple. Don't you agree?" Miranda stood behind me.

I turned to see who she referred to, which was obvious. "Blake and Eliza?" Miranda's smile reminded me of the Mona Lisa—sly—like she knew something I didn't. "I'm happy he's having a good time tonight. He's suffered enough over the past few years. Good to see him enjoying himself." He wasn't singing to Eliza. That brought me comfort. The song was his love song to me. Not her.

"Good to see but must be cause for uneasiness." Miranda smirked.

I pushed my shoulders back and lifted my chin. "Why? Is my job in jeopardy because Blake is smiling and having a good time?" Possibly came off as sarcasm which was not my intent.

She crinkled her nose. "No. Of course not. I thought . . . well, I've heard rumors related to you and Blake being involved."

I focused on her eyes. "Blake and I are involved in many things. We work well together and accomplish a great deal for BCH."

"Never mind. I have important people to talk to." She strutted off in a huff.

Beth, Tauni, and Allison were huddled together in the kitchen praying when I returned. I waited for them to finish. "Everything okay?"

Allison touched my arm. "We were praying for you. We heard the song and saw you follow Miranda into the room."

"I'm fine." Their love and concern overwhelmed me. A blessing for sure.

"I can't believe Miranda set you up like that." Tauni sounded angry. "Why is she hateful?"

"She has her own agenda." *Funny. Two months ago, Tauni acted like Miranda does now.*

I grabbed Jenny's arm when she hurried by. "What time is it? Are we anywhere close to 10:00?"

"Not yet—almost 9:00." She told me that she'd received a call from Carl a few minutes earlier.

All eyes turned to look at someone behind me. I spun and saw Blake. Everyone scattered to allow him a minute to talk with me in private.

He reached out to touch me but stopped himself. "Miranda approached the band and asked them to play our song. You know it's my song to you and you only?"

I nodded. "I know."

"And I want you to know this. I don't plan to see Eliza after tonight." He rubbed the back of his neck. "Hopefully, the couple of times she and I have been together were enough to stop some of the rumors. I may need to find someone else to date, though, before this is all over."

"What about one of those ladies who stopped us on our way to the worship center the first time you attended church with me? They're not *that* much older than you."

"I think I'll pass." He chuckled.

I loved to hear him laugh.

"Have you heard from Carl?" Blake's smile faded. "How's Nicki?"

"She woke up a few minutes ago and asked for Mama and Nana."

"You two go home and spend a few minutes with her. But before you go, I'd like to call her and sing 'Happy Birthday.' Can we do that now?"

"Here?"

"No. In my recording studio. Follow me upstairs."

"Recording studio?" What other non-necessary rooms did he have in his house?

"I keep my guitars and banjos in there."

"Someone could see us." I kept my voice low. "That's all we'd need. The rumors would escalate for sure."

He rubbed his chin. "Go up these stairs." He pointed to the staircase leading from the kitchen to the second floor. "When you reach the top, turn to the right and go to the second door on the left. Five minutes." He raised one hand. "I'll go up now using the front stairs."

I shook my head. "Not a good idea. People are roaming all throughout your house."

He sighed. "You're right. Bring someone with you. Jenny, Allison, Tauni, Beth. All of them. I want this to be a surprise for Nicki." He hurried away in the direction of the foyer and great room.

Five minutes later I grabbed Jenny and Tauni. They were excited to be my cohorts. We snuck up the back stairs. *Could I be fired for this? Not until Monday when the policy goes into effect.* We found the recording studio and slid inside.

I scanned the room. I'd never been in a real recording studio before, but this resembled what I'd seen on television. In the front of the room, near the door, was a small rectangular table with four chairs. Blake's guitars and banjos either rested in stands or were mounted on the walls. The recording equipment sat in front of the vocal booth, which was to the back of the studio behind large glass windows.

Blake picked up his guitar, tuned it, and looked at Jenny and me. "Would one of you call Nicki? I'll play and sing to her."

I clicked on Carl's number, put the phone on speaker, and asked if Nicki was awake. We all took a seat at the table.

Carl gave the phone to Nicki. "Hi, Nana. Where are you? I thought you were coming over tonight." She sounded weak and sad.

"I didn't want to disturb your sleep baby girl. What if we spend time together tomorrow?"

After a few seconds, Carl laughed. "She's nodding."

I smiled. "Mommy's here too."

"Hi, Mommy. I love you and miss you."

Jenny beamed. "I'll be home soon."

I peered into Blake's eyes. He watched everything I did. "Nana has a surprise for you. He's not Scotty Nelson, but someone wants to sing to you. Are you ready?"

Blake moved my cell closer to him. "Hi, Nicki. Happy Birthday."

"Papa Blake. I'm excited you called me on my birthday. I've waited all day for this."

"All day?"

"I knew my papa would call me today."

Jenny chuckled. Tauni's gaze darted around the table. The expression on her face was priceless. I held in my giggle.

Blake's mouth twisted to the side. "Would you like me to sing Happy Birthday?"

His rendition brought squeals of delight from Nicki. After chatting another minute, he disconnected the call. "I'm glad I was able to sing to her."

"She seemed excited. That's for sure." Jenny applauded. "And you have a fabulous voice."

Tauni stared at Blake. "I'm happy you included me in this. Papa Blake? And wow. I didn't know you sang and played guitar."

He set the instrument in a guitar stand and looked at Tauni. "I don't mind if you tell the whole world I know how to play the guitar and sing 'Happy Birthday.'" He lowered his voice. "But considering the current situation regarding a certain policy, please don't share anything concerning my new name."

I leaned closer to Tauni. "I've tried several times to tell Nicki that Blake is my boss. She insists on calling him Papa for a reason unknown to us."

Tauni's eyes sparkled. "Maybe she has a spiritual gift?"

116

Twelve

The next day, Sunday, at 5:00 p.m. we held Nicki's sixth birthday celebration with family. The evening before, I asked Wes if he'd like to join us if Nicki was feeling well enough. He was happy to accept. Shortly after we arrived at Jenny's, and introductions were made, Nicki whispered in my ear.

"Where's Papa Blake? Why didn't he come with you today?"

"Let's go to your room and talk." I asked Wes if he'd mind if I left him in the living room to admire the Christmas tree and led Nicki by the hand to her room. "Sweetie, Blake is Nana's boss. He's not your grandpa."

She stuck her fingers in her ears.

I didn't want to talk any louder, so I pried her fingers from one ear and held onto them. "We work together. He came to my house at Thanksgiving because his children were gone. I didn't want him to be all alone on a special day."

She pulled her hand from my grip. "He *is* my papa."

My granddaughter was persistent. That may suit her well one day, but today, I was tired. "No. He's not."

I spoke more sternly than necessary.

"You need faith. He's going to marry you and be my papa." She stuck out her lower lip and crossed her arms. "You wait and see."

I wiped perspiration from my forehead. "What about Mr. Wes? He brought you a special gift. I know you'll be happy. He's a nice man and Nana's friend. Wouldn't he make a good grandpa?" Although I didn't desire a close relationship with Wes, I did try to steer her away from her obsession with Blake. Jenny would have her hands full consoling Nicki and me both if God's "Let him go" was permanent.

"Maybe. For some other little girl. But Blake is *my* papa."

Jenny opened Nicki's door and stood in the doorway. "Are you ready, birthday girl?"

Nicki scrambled off her bed and ran out the door. The rest of our conversation would need to wait.

After we ate pizza, cake, and ice cream, Wes gave Nicki an iTunes card and a poster of Scotty. He knew she was disappointed when she didn't get to attend the Opry the night before. He told her she could download her favorite Scotty songs.

Nicki gaped at the card. She turned it over and wrinkled her nose. "How does music come out of this?" She stuck out her lips.

Carl chuckled and asked her to bring the card to him. He educated her on downloads. She selected a couple of songs and decided she needed her own phone. She loved the gifts but never called Wes papa.

~

At 7:00 on Monday morning, my doorbell rang. Jim with another rose. The same salmon color. Jim didn't stay long. He handed me the flower and took off. I placed the rose in a bud vase and set it on my coffee table in the living room.

I arrived at the office a few minutes before 8:00. When my computer came to life, an article, posted ten minutes earlier on our Intranet, glared at me. "New Employee Policy." I stared at my monitor.

I couldn't believe Miranda and Lance had won. Why didn't the board accept Chad's postponement? He fought the policy, didn't he? Which board members did Miranda or Lance own? I picked up a pencil and broke it in half. What a mess.

Blake entered our suite. "Let's talk in my office."

I stepped inside, and he closed the door. "Blake, should we shut the door? The policy posted this morning."

"We'll be fine. We need to talk privately." He pointed to a chair at his table.

I remained next to the door. He was being careless. He may have enough money to not need his job, but I needed mine. I opened the door against his wishes. "I can't afford to get fired."

"Fine. Now may we sit?"

I almost saluted him. He used that stern tone I'd often heard a few months before. I sat at his round table facing his desk, and he sat across from me.

He spoke in a quiet but frustrated tone. "I'd like you to resign. That way, we can continue to see each other."

I slumped back into the chair. "We've discussed this. I need more time to pray and seek the Lord. For now, we need to keep things on a professional basis." I closed my eyes.

Blake smacked the table. I jerked and snapped my eyes open. "We haven't discussed this. You have. Sounds like it's all about you."

I lifted my eyebrows and gaped at him. "I told you. This has nothing to do with me. What does God want?" I clasped my palms together and brought them to my chin. "I came to BCH believing I would never date—no plans to remarry. You changed that. But I can't jump into a commitment without prayerful consideration."

He ran his fingers through his hair but didn't speak. His right hand lingered on top of his head.

I reached across the table and briefly touched his left hand. "What happened after I left the party? Are you okay?"

He rubbed his eyes. "I'll never offer my home again for a party. People drank too much. Several spent the night. For a bunch of top dogs, they were wild."

"And Miranda? Did she behave herself?"

"Other than the time she asked you to bring dessert out."

"And Eliza?"

"Eliza's one of those who spent the night. She drank too much. Her daughter insisted she stay. We spent much of Sunday together."

Oh, no. "How did that happen?"

He leaned toward me. "I sense a little jealousy there." He crossed his arms and leaned back. "You should be jealous. If anything happens between Eliza and me, remember, this was your fault."

I plopped back in my chair and peered at him. My gut twisted. He thought this was easy for me. "Try to understand. I love you and want to be with you." I glanced at the open door. "But I'm waiting on the Lord to say, yes."

He shook his head. "You make me crazy." He stood and plodded over to his window and stared out. "Several on the board pulled me aside after you left and talked to me." My heart pounded louder in my chest. I stood and moved toward him. I could barely hear what he said. "The rumors continue to get worse. The board thinks if I openly date the rumors will lessen." He turned to face me. "They didn't insist, but I think it best if Eliza and I continue to see each other on a regular basis. However, if you decide to resign—"

"You and Eliza?" *He lied to me?* I shifted my weight to the opposite leg.

"Yes, I'm taking her to lunch again today. I thought you should know. I've asked her to wait for me in the lobby. No doubt she'll come up here anyway."

I scanned his office to gather my thoughts before I gawked at him. "You said after the holiday party you wouldn't see her again. Can't we put us on hold but not date anyone else?"

He came closer. Pain filled his eyes. "Maybe after a few weeks. But not now. Too much pressure with the new policy. I don't see any other way."

I gritted my teeth. "Date someone else. What about Tauni?"

"Tauni? She's dating Mitch. I told you before. You don't have any reason to be concerned regarding me and Eliza."

Yeah, right. I spun on my heels and returned to my desk. I clasped my hands together in my lap and stared at them. *Why Eliza?* Seeing her a couple of times confirmed Allison's and Beth's descriptions were accurate. Evil. A modern-day Jezebel. Dating others was not a part of this policy. Why did Blake think seeing that evil woman would help stifle rumors? She would only cause more. I lowered my head to my desk and closed my eyes.

Thirteen

Blake and I continued to face challenges throughout the week. We spoke and were kind to one another for the most part, but tension lingered between us. I couldn't relax and enjoy my work when he was nearby. He seemed off too. On occasion, he got snooty with me. Like the old Blake.

Tauni and I enjoyed lunch on Wednesday. We drove to a nearby restaurant and shared a pepperoni pizza.

She caught me up on her relationship with Mitch. "He's manipulative and demanding. I hoped he would dump me, but it looks like I need to be the mean one and break up with him."

We joined hands, and I asked the Lord to give her wisdom and guide her in how she should handle the situation. I also prayed that Mitch would understand and not cause a scene.

Wes and I lunched together on Thursday. I was gone an extra ten minutes, and Blake jumped all over me. When I checked my phone, I saw I'd never hit send on my text to him to let him know I was running late. I apologized and explained, but he was still upset.

On Friday afternoon while the office was quiet, I

hoped to improve my skills. I found and opened a recorded webinar called "Better Technology for Administrative Professionals," but I couldn't get the sound to work. After trying everything I could think of to hear the webinar, I called our IT Department.

Wes answered my call. After I told him my problem, he said he'd be up to check soon.

A few minutes later, Blake called me into his office. "Has anything changed?"

I sat across from his desk. "There appears to be more tension between us this week."

"I agree. But that's not what I asked." He sounded annoyed. "Have you changed your mind regarding us?" He spoke in a sarcastic tone. "Have you heard from God, yet?"

Blake still didn't get it. I was drained. I continued to skip meals and prayed frequently. "You're waiting on me, and I'm waiting on you." I tried to sound pleasant. "Our relationship and the possibility of getting married is mainly between you and God now, not me and God." I failed with the pleasantry.

"What are you saying?" He scowled. "I attend church, read my Bible, counsel with Manuel, listen to *your* music, and pray. Not enough for you? Do you want to manipulate everything I do?"

I stood and placed my hands on my hips. "Who are you doing those things for? Me? They're not for me." I brushed my bangs off to the side. "I want you to do them for the Lord and because you find pleasure in them and in Him." I zipped out his door. I hated what this policy had done to us.

Blake followed close behind. "This is crazy." He raised his hands and brought them back down. "I've been patient with you. Understanding too. But this has gone on long enough. Eliza won't put all this religious nonsense on me. She'll marry me in a heartbeat."

My breath caught in my throat, and I reeled around to face him. "Marry you?" I placed my hand on my chest.

Wes rushed into our suite. "Religious nonsense?" He closed the door behind him.

I looked at Wes, shook my head, and lifted my palm to caution him.

He ignored me. "Blake needs to hear this from someone other than you." He glared at Blake. "Keedryn needs a husband who leads. Someone who is the spiritual head of the household. To take his rightful place in the home. A man who follows Christ."

Blake clenched his fists. I stepped in between the two men and stared at Blake.

Wes wasn't finished. "Let go of your pride, or you'll lose her forever."

With my back to him, I held my hand behind me, waving at him to stop. Couldn't Wes see Blake's reddened face?

"Truth be told, I'd like her to dump you and be my girl." Wes pressed on. "But you hold her heart. After God that is. He's first with her. Right where He should be."

Blake crowded in between Wes and me. I turned to watch.

Blake stood face to face with Wes. "Sounds like you're the husband she needs. I give her to you. You can have her."

I took a step back and bumped against a wall. I tried to grip something, anything. Nothing there to hold onto. I wasn't sure I could stand. I closed my eyes to stop the spinning.

"The two of you can serve God and live happily ever after." Blake spewed. "I have a lady waiting on me who'll love me for who I am whether I decide to serve the Lord or not. She has no ulterior motives."

I opened my eyes and saw Blake bump hard into Wes on his way out the door.

Wes helped me to my chair. "I can't believe he blew up like that. Are you okay?"

I nodded. I wasn't okay, though. I didn't know what was worse. God telling me to let Blake go or Blake giving me to Wes like I meant nothing to him.

Wes knelt in front of me and took both of my hands in his. He prayed a beautiful prayer over me. He also prayed for Blake. After his prayer, he lingered. "I'm not going to leave you until I know you're okay."

"I'm fine." I stared at the wall in front of me.

Wes didn't budge.

I wanted him to leave so I could cry alone. I clutched my stomach. *Blake didn't walk out on me. Did he? Marry Eliza? Impossible.*

I blinked my tears away and looked at Wes. "You should go. I don't want you to get in trouble for not getting your work done."

"Making sure you're okay is more important than my work." He stood and grabbed a few tissues from my desk and handed them to me. "Would you like company this evening?"

I sniffled. "Nicki's spending the night. I promised to take her out to see Christmas lights this evening and shop for her parents in the morning." I stood. I was grateful for Wes's concern, prayers, and friendship. So much so, I did something I shouldn't have done. I hugged him—a quick, thank-you hug.

Miranda strutted in. "What have we here? Keedryn and Wes." She strolled over to Blake's office and peeked inside. "I hoped to catch Blake. Is he here?"

When her back was to us, Wes grabbed my hand. I gave him a sidelong glance.

I took a deep breath and kept my voice steady. "He left for the day. Would you like to leave him a message?"

"I'll check with him later."

Wes turned to face me. "I'll pick you up at 6:00. Will that work?"

Cute. He wanted to rescue me from rumors. "That'll be perfect. Nicki will enjoy seeing you again."

I peered at Miranda. "We're taking my granddaughter out to see Christmas lights tonight."

"How sweet." She glared at Wes. "Don't you have a job to do?"

"Yep. I'm gone." He squeezed my hand and leaned toward my ear. "I'll see you later."

When Wes left, Miranda stepped closer. "Did he kiss you on the cheek?"

"Would that be a problem if he did? We don't work in the same department." If she wanted a fight, I was ready.

"Are the two of you getting serious?"

"I suppose that depends on your definition of serious. We've been seeing each other for the past three months." I didn't lie, but I didn't admit to any dates. We ate lunch together often.

"Hmm. Your relationship with Wes isn't a fake?"

I reached across my desk to turn off my computer.

"Wes is a great guy. We enjoy one another's company."

"And is Blake serious about Eliza?"

"Sounds that way. I guess if you want to know more, you can ask him."

"And you're okay with that?"

I wanted to wipe the sneer off her face. "Blake is free to date whomever he wishes. Forgive me. But I'm getting tired of all the questions, and I need to leave early today."

~

I called Jenny and asked if she could bring Nicki to my place instead of me stopping by to pick her up after work. I needed an hour of alone time to pull myself together. Blake broke my heart.

You can have her, Wes. I give her to you.

I laid across my bed, wept, and prayed. Blake sounded angry and hateful. He spoke ugly to me and Wes. How could he act that way toward me? If that was the way he loved, I was better off without him.

Jenny dropped Nicki off at 5:45 p.m. My granddaughter asked me why my Christmas tree lights weren't on and told me I needed more decorations.

"I had more at the bottom, but Roxie keeps knocking them off. She's broken two already, so I moved the others higher."

Nicki laughed. "She and Lucy would have fun together."

Wes arrived at 6:00. Nicki was excited when she saw him, although she questioned me before he came as to why Blake wouldn't join us.

After I grabbed our coats from the hallway closet, Wes drove us across town to a drive-through dancing light show. We tuned the radio to the correct frequency and enjoyed flashing lights while listening to "Jingle Bells," "Deck the Halls," "Up on the Housetop," and several other fun songs. Lights of many colors and designs danced to the beat of the music.

Nicki couldn't contain her excitement. "These are the best Christmas lights I've ever seen. Can we drive through again?" She pointed and squealed with delight at everything.

Wes laughed. "Have you toured the Gaylord Opryland Hotel this time of year?"

"I have." I turned to see Nicki behind me. "Have you ever gone with Mommy and Daddy?"

Her eyes grew round. "Do they have pretty lights too?"

Wes said, "You bet. Decorated trees, flashing lights, snowmen, and other decorations."

"Can we go tonight?" Nicki bounced in her car seat.

I looked at Wes and he chuckled. Now I needed to add something else to my Saturday to-do list. I told Nicki we'd try to go after we finished shopping for her parents in the morning. We could have lunch at the mall and afterward go to the hotel. She invited Wes to join us. He was thrilled but not excited enough to shop. We made plans, while we drove back to my condo, to meet him at the Gaylord. He dropped us off in time for Nicki to get a bath and go to bed.

There were two things I needed to do before I turned in for the night. First, discard the rose Jim delivered on Monday. I lifted the bud vase from my coffee table and plodded into the kitchen. When I pulled the flower out of its vase, I brought the fragrant petals to my nose. No more roses. No more Blake.

After a couple of minutes holding the flower close to my heart, I tossed it into the trash. *I'm no longer his one-and-only.*

I shuffled to my bedroom and used my laptop to prepare my resignation letter. I couldn't stay at BCH after what he said and did today, especially if he married Eliza.

~

On Saturday morning, three days before Christmas, Nicki and I attempted the impossible. We drove to Opry Mills Mall. Traffic slowed on Briley Parkway, and the exit ramp was bumper to bumper. Finding a parking spot was worse. Nicki jumped up and down when we entered the mall. She enjoyed the kiosks the best, especially the toy helicopter circling above her head. We fought our way through the crowd. Thankfully, Nicki didn't complain. She persisted in finding the perfect gifts for Jenny and Carl. She also insisted on a Santa hat for Mr. Wes. He was thrilled when she gave it to him that afternoon. He wore it while we toured the Gaylord Opryland.

We entered the Delta Atrium of the Gaylord—an indoor village of shops, restaurants, plants, trees, fountains, and a winding stream beneath a glass roof. We were greeted with festive lights aglow, decorations of all sizes and shapes, and the Delta Riverboat. Nicki loved the large candy canes and snowmen. There were crowds everywhere enjoying the lights and Christmas music.

We made our way to the Cascades Atrium—an indoor garden complete with a fishpond and a gushing waterfall. Poinsettias galore added to the beauty. Nicki was in awe of the koi. We were enjoying the fish when

Nicki broke loose of my hand.

"Nicki, come back." With Wes on my heels, I hurried after her. She ran farther away from me toward the waterfall. I halted and watched as Blake got down on his knees to catch her in his arms. She smothered him with kisses and hugged his neck. He picked her up and held her close before he turned in my direction. Behind him stood Eliza glaring at me with cold, dark eyes.

I trudged toward them but kept my focus on Nicki. "She sprinted all the way to you." I patted her on the back. "Sweetie, you need to come with Nana now. Mr. Blake is busy." When I placed both hands near her waist to remove her from Blake's arms, she buried her face into his neck. I eyed Blake staring at me.

Eliza, wearing a scowl, crossed her arms and let out a loud breath. "Who is this *adorable* child?"

Blake's eyes narrowed and he glared at Eliza. "There's an available bench over there." He pointed in the direction of the bench. "Go save us a seat."

She remained behind him. Couldn't blame her with me, the former rival, in her space.

Blake's eyes softened when he peered at me. "Eliza's niece just finished singing a solo with her school choir. We came to support her."

"Nice." I pulled at Nicki's waist again. "Mr. Blake's busy. We need to go."

"Nicki's no bother. I'm happy to see her and happy she still enjoys seeing me." He stared past me. "You're here with Wes?"

I nodded and looked at Nicki. "Come Nicki. We need to finish up and get you home soon." This time she reached for me, and I put her down on the walkway.

She took my hand and gazed up at Blake. "Bye, Papa. I love you."

I peeked at Eliza. She glowered back at me. Evil personified. A chill ran down my spine.

Nicki and I turned toward Wes. When I glanced at her, she twisted her body toward Blake and threw him a kiss. Of all the people living in the Nashville area what was the chance I'd run into him? *Why God?*

Wes took my free hand. "Are you okay?"

Not at all. "Can we leave? I don't want to run into them again."

On our way back we stopped for ice cream. After we finished our treat, Nicki asked if we could ride the riverboat.

"Are you up for it?" Wes whispered in my ear.

"If the line's not too long."

We took the stairs down to the boarding area. Nicki tried to let go of my hand, but I held tight. I followed her gaze and saw Blake and Eliza in line. One couple would be between us. A strong possibility we'd be in the same boat. Since we were still several feet away from them, I put my arm in front of Wes and gave a nod in their direction.

Wes stopped. "Maybe we can do this another time."

I gazed at Nicki. "Another day, sweetie. We need to leave now."

She whined and Blake turned toward us. I spun toward the walkway and pulled Nicki behind me. Wes reached down and picked up a wiggly six-year-old who insisted on winning this battle. She lost. He carried her over to a fountain converted into a huge decorated Christmas tree and sat her down. He offered her a few coins to throw into the winding riverboat stream. She pouted but agreed. We followed her to the water's edge.

I turned to Wes. "Great diversion. You must have experience with grandchildren." He embraced me and smacked me with a kiss. I stepped back with wide eyes.

He put his lips close to my ear. "I saw Terri from Legal and thought it might help to counter the rumors."

"Thanks." *I think.*

I glanced over my shoulder to check on Nicki. She held a coin out in front of her and closed her eyes. When she snapped open her eyes, she giggled and tossed the coin into the water.

Wes touched my shoulder. "Why are you doing this to yourself? Why do you allow Blake to hurt you over and over? He doesn't deserve you or your love. I'd treat you as a gift from God."

I scanned the area to see if Terri was nearby. Did he lie to me about her, too, so he could kiss me? I focused on Wes. "Do we deserve anyone's love? Do we deserve God's? He gives His freely. Am I to hold back mine from Blake because he's not living the way I think he should? That's not how God works." I shook my head. "I'm sorry, Wes. I'm in love with Blake." Wes flinched and the color drained from his face.

He looked over at Nicki and called her name. "I'm leaving now. Merry Christmas."

She waved goodbye and turned to me. "Can we go see Papa Blake again?"

Fourteen

After church on Sunday I drove to Jenny's for lunch.

She treated me as if I were a piece of fine china—delicate and breakable. She held my elbow and strolled alongside of me to the dining room table. She fussed over me and told me I didn't look well.

How should I look? Broken? Hurt? That's me. I couldn't find relief from my nausea. I'd lost Blake and now my friend, Wes, whom I hurt again. *I must be a terrible person.*

When Nicki saw me, she ran over and hugged me. "I didn't hear you come in. Where's Papa Blake? Will he be here later?"

I didn't need this today. When I saw him at the hotel, his only concern was for Nicki. None for me whatsoever. I accepted we were done. Nicki needed to understand too. I spoke in a harsh tone. "I told you before. He's *not* your grandpa."

"You're mad at me." Tears fell down her cheeks.

I didn't know how she could turn them on so quickly.

"Why don't you believe me? Don't you like him?"

Jenny understood my exasperation even if Nicki

didn't. "Go pick up your toys. We can talk about this later."

Nicki scurried off muttering to herself.

Jenny called her back. "Young lady. Are you sassing your mother?"

"No, Mama. I wasn't talking to you. I was talking to Jesus. I asked Him to help Nana believe Papa Blake is *my* papa." She scampered down the hallway and into her room humming a Veggie Tales song.

I sighed. "Let her go." I held my forehead. "She's adamant about this. I don't get it, but apparently she does."

"Let's eat. I'll put her down for her quiet time, and we can talk without interruption. I have an idea to bounce off you. I think you'll need to take a step of faith, but it might open Blake's heart all the way to God."

"I'm intrigued." I didn't have the heart to tell her Blake and I were finished. To tell her now would hold up our meal, and she and Carl had everything ready.

Lunch was flavorless—what little I ate. But it was good to spend the afternoon with family. Jenny shared old memories of her college friends. Made me laugh. Laughter does do us good. Medicine for the soul.

We also shared memories that caused me to miss Sam. I told Nicki, "You loved to climb into Grandpa Sam's lap and comb his hair. He'd tear up because your mama would get in his lap, too, and comb his hair when she was a little girl."

After Jenny put Nicki down to rest, and I cleaned up the kitchen, Jenny and I retired to the living room. I sat on the sofa and she in her favorite chair. Carl excused himself to the bonus room to wrap Christmas gifts.

Jenny questioned me concerning my prayers and asked if I'd sensed the Lord directing me to marry Blake. I shared with her that Wes preached to Blake on Friday afternoon and Blake's response.

She gaped at me and touched the base of her neck. "Marry Eliza after one week?" She shook her head. "That's crazy."

"What's your idea?"

"I don't think it matters now. I think you should turn your attention to Wes. I like him."

"I'd like to hear what you wanted to tell me." I glanced at the floor. "Not that it will make any difference. But I'm curious."

She took a deep breath. "What if you go ahead and accept Blake's proposal?" She grinned like this was the greatest idea. Ever.

"That's the best you can do?" I peered at her, open-mouthed for a moment.

"You've been Jesus to him. You've shown him love, acceptance, and forgiveness. But what if he doesn't feel that acceptance because you haven't been able to commit yourself to him?"

"I doubt I've done a good job of being Jesus to him or we wouldn't be in this mess." I stared at a picture of Nicki on the wall. "But I have loved him. Forgiveness will be hard. He's hurt me many times." I brought my legs up close to my body and hugged them.

"He may need your commitment to believe he can receive the Lord's forgiveness, acceptance, and love." Jenny joined me on the sofa.

"I'm not following."

"Maybe he thinks he must clean up and be perfect

for you. That's a lot of pressure." Jenny called Lucy over. The dog needed a bath. "We don't clean up before coming to Christ. Although a lot of people think they need to. He wants us and accepts us the way we are." Jenny tilted her head. "Following now?"

I nodded and rubbed Lucy behind the ears. "I love you dog. Even if you do smell."

"We come first." Jenny patted my knee. "And He does His work in us."

"Blake did accuse me of trying to manipulate him." I leaned forward and gazed out the window.

Jenny put her arm across my shoulder and squeezed. "Continue to be Jesus to him. Accept him for who he is now. He knows the Lord. He's a believer. A struggling believer. But Carl talked to him on Thanksgiving. And he thinks Blake loves God. He's going through a rough spot."

"There's a problem with what you're suggesting."

"I know that now. He's marrying Eliza. That's why I said, 'I like Wes.'"

"When I consider Blake and Eliza together, I realize I don't know him at all. How could he think she'd make him happy?" I closed my eyes and leaned back. "But I'm certain Wes isn't the man for me." Lucy jumped into my lap. I scrunched my nose and put her back on the floor. "There's another problem with your idea."

"What?"

"God hasn't told me to accept Blake's proposal." I stood and trudged over to where I'd left my purse. I was restless. Maybe a drive would help. I turned to face her. "The Lord told me to 'Let him go.'"

"And He's now telling you to marry Blake." She

jumped up and plastered on that silly grin of hers.

I chuckled at her lightheartedness, although tears puddled in my eyes. "What do you mean? He hasn't told me that."

"Nicki."

"What?"

"She's probably not asleep. Let's go see her." She grabbed my hand and pulled me down the hallway. I dropped my purse. Didn't look like I'd be leaving any time soon.

Nicki sat on her bed, reading a Bible storybook. "I'm reading 'bout Jesus. He helps me with the words."

Sweet and innocent.

Jenny sat on the bed. "Tell Nana what you told me about Jesus and Papa Blake."

I gazed up at the ceiling and back to my two girls sitting on the bed.

"I don't think so Mama. Nana doesn't believe me. She doesn't have enough faith to hear yet."

"Now wait a moment young lady." I smiled to make sure she knew I wasn't upset with her. "I have plenty of faith."

"Then you should believe me." She sprang from her bed and grabbed my hand. "I told you that Jesus said you and Papa Blake are getting married soon. Jesus doesn't tell me lies." She pulled me over to the bed, pushed me down, and sat next to me.

I rubbed my arms. "Jesus told you? He told you we're going to get married?" Not only her expression but the tone of her voice. Certainty? Faith? She believed every word she spoke.

"That's what I said. Because that's what He said. You wear me out, Nana. I'm tired." She crawled under her covers, rolled to her side, and closed her eyes.

Jenny rubbed her back.

Nicki popped open her eyes and sat up. "I forgot. Something else Jesus told me."

Jenny and I both stared at her. "What?"

"Mommy has a baby in her tummy." She made a pouty face.

Jenny's head jerked toward me. Her eyes teared up. "Baby?" She peered at Nicki. "Why are you sad? I thought you wanted a brother or sister."

"I only want a sister." She wasn't good at hiding disappointment. She sounded irritated. "But Jesus said no. This time a brother."

Jenny jumped up and pulled me into the hallway. "I'm running to Walgreens. I'll also pick up mints. That's what you can tell Carl. I needed mints. I'll be back in a few minutes."

She hurried out the door in a flash.

When Jenny returned, she pulled me into the bathroom. "You know what this means, if the pregnancy test is positive?"

I clapped. "I'm going to have a grandson."

"No. Well, yes. But it also means you're going to marry Blake."

Fifteen

I'm going to marry Blake. Seemed impossible after he said he was done with me. Who would give away a woman you claimed to love? I wasn't sure I wanted him any longer. He broke my heart. Would our marriage continue to bring this kind of pain and heartache?

Before I turned in for the night, I knelt beside my bed. Was the Lord saying I could marry Blake? I didn't want to mess this up. Should I listen to the counsel of a six-year-old?

Lord, I surrender myself to You. I release every misconception I have of who You are, what Your plans are for me, and who you work through to convey Your plans. Please confirm what you want me to do. I need to forgive Blake for the brokenness he's caused me. If I can't forgive him, I certainly can't marry him. Help me.

~

Monday morning, but more importantly, Christmas Eve. The office was closed until Wednesday. I needed further counsel and called Manuel. We agreed to meet at Starbucks. His wife Susie joined us.

We found a table and chatted for a few minutes before Manuel said, "I was surprised by your call and what you want to discuss."

I stared at my hands and picked at my fingernails. "Why does that surprise you?" I focused on Manuel. "I believe the Lord's given me the okay to marry Blake." I peered down at my lap. "But I'm not certain that's what I want anymore. I'll need to first forgive him for wounding my heart. I'm not sure I'm ready." I bit my lower lip and made eye contact again.

Manuel and Susie looked at one another. He cleared his throat. "I'm under the impression Blake's seeing someone else and getting serious enough to discuss marriage."

I winced. "Are you still counseling him?"

Manuel nodded.

I shared what Blake said to Wes and me on Friday. Manuel was aware of the conversation. He and Blake met on Saturday. A good sign—Blake was still seeking God.

I shook my head. "He doesn't love Eliza. He's making a huge mistake."

Manuel frowned and leaned toward me. "I don't believe he loves her either. Although, he hasn't admitted that to me." He took a sip of his latte. "What's happened for you to think the Lord has given you the go ahead?"

I shared how Nicki calls Blake Papa and her knowledge of the new baby. Manuel reminded me that God can speak through anyone. He also encouraged me to forgive Blake soon.

When Manuel excused himself to the restroom, Susie touched my hand. "Be careful. Sounds like Blake's convinced he's doing this for you."

"Planning to marry Eliza for me?" I pointed to my

chest. "Doesn't he realize how he's hurt me because of her?"

She squeezed my hand. "Blake feels he's not good enough for you." She glanced around and spoke in a whisper. "He thinks Wes would make you a better husband. You have a lot of work to do to convince him otherwise. He loves you enough to let you go."

I gawked at Susie with my mouth opened. "Did Manuel tell you this?"

She crinkled her nose. "I was in the adjoining office sorting through files. I overheard things. Manuel doesn't know."

I patted her hand, grabbed my purse and jacket, and asked her to thank Manuel for me.

I wrestled over what to do on my drive home. When should I talk to Blake? When I drop off Andy and Zoey? But what about Eliza? I was sure she'd be at Blake's house for Christmas. And I needed to forgive him first. What would I say? *Hi, Blake. I'm ready to commit. Marry me, and we'll live happily ever after.* I didn't want to marry him any longer. How did everything get so complicated?

After I prayed throughout the day, it didn't feel right for me to call Blake. Instead, I would trust the timing to the Lord.

~

Christmas morning was too quiet. I invited Jenny and her family for lunch to allow them time in the morning to open their gifts. Too early to begin cooking, since I didn't prepare a huge Christmas meal like I did for Thanksgiving. Today we would have enchiladas—chicken and cheese.

I sat on the sofa in the TV room with Roxie curled

up beside me. *Not supposed to be like this.* I missed Sam, and Blake was celebrating Christmas with Eliza when he should have been with me. I got up and wandered to the kitchen to eat breakfast, opened the refrigerator, stared inside, and closed the door without taking anything out. I rubbed the back of my neck and returned to the sofa.

A ping from my cell. *Maybe Blake?* I pulled the phone out of my pocket. A text from Wes. "Merry Christmas." I sent one back to him with the same message.

Roxie crawled into my lap and purred her content, but I found little comfort in her affection. I shivered. *I may see Blake tonight when I drop off Andy and Zoey. Seeing him could be worse today than Friday at work.* I rubbed my hands together to stop the shaking.

The temperature was mild for December. Mid-forties. I grabbed my coat, headed outdoors, and strolled through the neighborhood while I prayed. When I returned to my condo, I focused on lunch preparations.

At noon, Nicki came running inside excited to see me. Or so I thought.

"Where's Papa Blake? Isn't he here yet?"

"Blake's not coming today, honey. Did Jesus tell you that he would be here?"

"No." She pouted. "I hoped he would come over for Christmas."

After lunch, we gathered in the living room to open gifts and sing a few carols. Carl carried on Sam's tradition and read from Chapter Two of Luke. Nicki led us in "Silent Night."

Our afternoon flew by. At 3:00 I reminded them

that I needed to head to the airport soon.

Jenny took Nicki's hand. "We need to go now. Nana needs to leave."

"Nana. Where are you going on your trip?"

"I'm not going anywhere. I'm picking up Blake's son and his girlfriend and taking them to Blake's house. My Christmas gift to Blake's family."

"They don't live with him?"

"They live far away in New Mexico. They're coming here for a surprise visit. Blake isn't expecting them."

Her eyes got big. "He'll be happy to see them. And to see you too."

Her exuberance blessed my heart. "He will be happy to see them."

"Can I come with you? I want to see them too."

Jenny pulled Nicki toward the front door. "Let's go home. You need to pick up your toys and help Mama bake cookies."

"Yay. Cookies. I love to bake cookies. Bye, Nana." She looked at her daddy. "Are you going to help us bake too?"

He nodded, and they said their good-byes.

I prayed all the way to the airport. I asked the Lord to let me drop Andy and Zoey off with little or no interaction with Blake or Eliza.

Sixteen

I waited for Andy and Zoey in the baggage claim area. My stomach ached. A strong possibility I'd see Blake an hour from now. I didn't want to see him with her. Not again. Saturday was hard enough. I opened my purse and took out my wallet. How much cash did I have? Enough for Andy and Zoey to take a taxi? I sighed. That was a stupid idea. I'd face Blake sooner or later at the office. Why put it off?

There weren't as many flights on Christmas Day as other times of the year. However, at 4:30 in the afternoon, people seemed weary. I smiled at the people making their way down the escalator. The day of celebrating my Savior's birth—a happy face wouldn't kill me. When I caught sight of Andy and Zoey my smile grew to a toothy grin. I greeted them both with a hug, pulled away, and looked at Andy. "Your dad will be thrilled. Did you talk with him today?"

Andy nodded. The dimple in his chin, reminded me of Blake. "He called this morning. His 'Merry Christmas' sounded grumpy." He took Zoey's hand.

"Hopefully, things will get better when he sees the two of you." I led the way to the carousel to retrieve their bags. "Did he say when Allison and Jim are coming over?"

Zoey grimaced. "You mean the two of you didn't get together today?" Her lower lip jutted out.

Her forlorn expression made me want to cry. "I haven't seen him." I took in the similar suitcases drifting by before turning my attention back to Zoey.

Her shoulders drooped. "But today's Christmas. You plan to stay when we get to the house, don't you? And you're still dating, aren't you?"

"We dated one time. After that, everything fell apart."

"That can't be." Zoey grabbed Andy's arm. "Andy?"

I was surprised by her reaction. "What's wrong?"

Andy gathered up their luggage, a suitcase on wheels and a duffle bag, and we walked outside to my car. I kept glancing over at Zoey. She appeared too emotional to speak.

"We have an announcement to make." Andy stopped, dropped his duffle bag, and wrapped his arm across Zoey's shoulder. "We're getting married."

I clasped my hands together. "That's wonderful. I'm happy for you. When's the big day?"

"We're hoping to get married this week," Zoey said through tears.

"What a lovely idea. But why are you crying?"

She shook her head.

We loaded the luggage into the trunk of my sedan and climbed into the car. Zoey rode in the front and Andy in the back.

Zoey sniffled. "I hoped you'd agree to be my Maid of Honor. And Andy wants his dad to be his Best Man. If you and Blake aren't dating any more, won't that be awkward?"

After paying the parking fee, I took the entrance ramp to I-40 West to make my way to the Brentwood area.

"I assure you we can be civil with one another." With my two-week resignation notice, we wouldn't need to be polite much longer. I'd be out of his life for good.

"But I thought maybe we could have a double ceremony." She wiped her eyes. "I was sure you two would get married soon. Since you both were married before, I didn't think you'd want a big wedding or need to put it off for several months."

I focused on the roadway. A double wedding? After one date? "If you want me in your wedding, I'll be there." I glanced at Zoey and she raised her eyebrows. I returned my focus to the road. "Blake and I work together five days a week. We'll not ruin your day." I frowned. "But there won't be a double wedding."

"I'm sorry. I've been a little emotional lately."

"She's been a lot emotional lately." Andy chuckled from the back seat.

"Hush." She turned and faced him with a scowl.

I peeked at Zoey. "Won't your family be disappointed they'll not be able to attend your wedding?"

"Just my mom. She disowned me a few months ago when she found out I was pregnant." She stared out the passenger side window. "She wanted me to get an abortion."

I flinched. "I'm sorry." Her mom and my Aunt Mary would have gotten along well. My aunt pressured my mom to abort me. I was grateful Mama didn't heed Aunt Mary's advice.

"No big deal." Zoey quickly dabbed her eyes again. "We were never close."

During our forty-five-minute drive to Blake's house, we chatted about the weather and the zero percent chance of snow expected while they were in town. We also discussed what they hoped to do or see while in Nashville as well as their wedding.

My chest tightened when I pulled into Blake's circular driveway at 6:00 p.m. The house was aglow with Christmas lights. I stopped the car midway up the drive for a couple of minutes for Zoey to get a good look.

She gazed at the house through the windshield. "Andy. You said the house was big. You didn't tell me huge." Her mouth fell open, and her head moved from the left to the right as she took everything in. "The Christmas lights are amazing. I love the glowing fountain the best." She turned to see Andy. "No other yard lights?"

"No. Dad never wanted to go overboard and have people stop on the road to gawk at the house."

I pulled up and parked in front of Blake's door. "Wait until you see the inside. Even more amazing. A magnificent house. We held the executive's holiday party here ten days ago." *When Blake was still willing to wait for me.*

Zoey glanced out the passenger window. "The wreath on the front door is beautiful too."

While she talked, I got out and opened my trunk— thankful no one on the inside noticed us. When I put the last bag on the driveway, an alarm sounded. Great. Now

I couldn't sneak away.

Allison opened the front door and let out a scream. "Is that my goofy bro?"

Blake, Eliza, and Jim followed her outdoors. I closed my trunk and trudged to the driver's side of my car. I heard footsteps behind me and turned to see Allison. She spun me around and wrapped me in her arms. "This is such a blessing."

"Merry Christmas." I embraced her in a big squeeze. "Tell your dad, Merry Christmas for me. I need to run." I saw her son standing fifteen feet away with the rest of the family near the front door. Tim's hair was light and wavy. He wore jeans and a red polo shirt. I wanted to leave but hesitated. "Could I meet Tim?"

Allison called him over.

Blake smiled and placed his arm across Andy's shoulder.

"This whole thing is crazy." Allison kept her voice low. "That woman is nuts. I can't stand to be in the same room with her. This must end soon. She's disgusting."

I placed my hand on Allison's arm. "Give her a chance. She may love your dad. And if she makes him happy, that's a good thing." I pulled my hand away.

Her lower lip quivered. "What are you saying? I don't understand. This separation is temporary? The policy?" She sounded horrified. "You two are trying to work everything out, and you'll be back together soon."

Tim scurried over and stuck out his hand. "Hi. I'm Tim. Nice to meet you."

"What a fine gentleman. Happy to meet you too."

After I shook his hand, he ran to where his dad

stood and stared up at Andy and Zoey.

Allison gawked at me. "Well? You two are working things out?"

"Doesn't seem likely." I observed Blake with his arm still across Andy's shoulder. Eliza's arms encircled Blake's waist. "I've got to run. Best if I don't have to talk to your dad tonight. Call me tomorrow. We'll talk." I hugged her and opened my car door. "I love you."

"Keedryn." Blake called out. "Wait."

I turned toward the front door and tried to swallow the sour taste in my mouth.

Blake said something to his family that I couldn't hear.

Tim opened the door, and the rest of the family followed him inside. Eliza lingered. She grabbed Blake's elbow. His demeanor changed, and he abruptly turned to her. I couldn't hear what he told her, but he pointed to the door. She glared at me before she made her way into the house.

I should have left. We could have dealt with this when we got back to work. What kept me there?

Blake took a few steps toward me to close the gap between us. "You did this for me?" He shook his head. "Arranged for Andy to come home for Christmas?"

I peered into his eyes. "For you and Allison. And for Andy and Zoey. A family needs to be together on Christmas." My body trembled. *What should I say? Help me.*

He moved another step closer. "This is a wonderful gift." He cleared his throat. "You know it's over, though, don't you?"

The coolness of the air. The iciness in his tone. I'd never been a fan of winter. Liked it less now.

"Eliza and I got engaged today." He paused. "When I go back inside, we'll tell the family."

I stiffened. The news didn't surprise me. Four days earlier, he told me this would happen. Manuel and Susie cautioned me as well. However, to hear of the official engagement from Blake devastated me. How did this happen so fast? I didn't get to tell him about Nicki talking to Jesus or how I was ready to commit.

I stared at the fountain behind him before I focused my attention back on his eyes. I needed to regain my composure. "My resignation will be on your desk tomorrow morning."

He jerked his head back. "Too late. Not going to work out between us."

"I understand. I'm not resigning for you to stop seeing Eliza or for us to be together."

"You're not?"

My heartrate increased. "I believe you think marrying Eliza is the best for me." My tone was deep and sharp. "I disagree. But you've made your choice. I know I can't stay at BCH." I gave a nod toward his front door. "I doubt she'd allow me to stay on as your assistant either."

He started to speak. But stopped.

I softened my demeanor, reached up, took his left cheek in my hand, and softly kissed his right. A tear met my lips. Not mine. I stepped back, gazed deep into his eyes, smiled, and whispered. "Merry Christmas, Blake. I love you." My voice caught. "You've become my one-and-only."

154

Seventeen

How I managed to do and say what I did without crying was a God thing. Amazed I told him that I loved him, and he was my one-and-only. *How can I still love him?* I turned away and got into my car.

Blake stopped my door from closing. "I've become your one-and-only?" Disbelief and softness in his voice. "I saw you from the riverboat. You kissed Wes."

I focused on his eyes again and shook my head. "You saw him kiss me. Unexpected and uninvited."

"But he's good for you." Blake stepped back, which I took to mean he was done with me.

I pulled the door closed, started the car, and put down my window. I peered up at him. "But I'm not in love with Wes." I drove away and headed home.

Near my house, I received a call from Jenny. She asked if I could stop by and pick up a picture Nicki drew for Blake's Christmas gift. She hoped I would take it to the office the next morning.

Jenny met me in her driveway with Nicki's envelope. I told her about my conversation with Blake and his engagement to Eliza. She hugged me close and prayed a quick prayer for strength and wisdom.

Blake confirmed there was no future for us. Nicki

insisted on Sunday there was. *What now? I'm ready to let him go. But is that still Your plan, Lord?*

~

Seldom did I hit the snooze button. Most often I woke up before the alarm went off. But today, the day after Christmas, I awoke thirty minutes late.

Making up thirty minutes was tough with everything I needed to do to get ready. I didn't like to be late for work. When I was almost caught up, the doorbell rang at 7:00. Who would be at my door so early? Couldn't be another flower delivery.

Jim? He held a single salmon colored rose. On the day after Blake and Eliza's engagement?

Does that man have any kind of brain in his head?

I yanked open the door and glared at Jim.

He took a step back and raised his palm toward me. "I'm only the courier. Don't shoot."

"Why is he doing this to me?" I held the door open for Jim to come inside.

"No time for a visit," he said, stammering. "I've got to run. Allison's expecting me."

"I'll text her and tell her that I kidnapped you for a few minutes." I reached for his arm. "Now. Get in here." After I yanked him inside without much of a fight, I lowered my eyebrows and squinted at him. "You're going to tell me what Blake wants from me."

Jim shrugged and gave me a lopsided grin. "I'm as dumbfounded as you are. He told me yesterday afternoon before Andy and Zoey arrived there'd be no more flowers." He sighed. "This morning Blake called and said, 'Extremely important you deliver Keedryn a rose this morning.'" He extended the flower.

"I don't want it." I pushed his hand away. "Tell

Blake whatever you want. This must stop."

"When Blake handed me the rose this morning, he said he wanted me to call him and let him know your reaction." He rubbed the back of his neck. "You want me to tell him 'This must stop?'"

"Why would he care how I react? This makes no sense to me." I shook my head and crossed my arms. "He made it perfectly clear Friday and yesterday he wanted nothing more to do with me."

Jim tilted his head from side to side. "A guess here." He tried again to hand me the flower. "Maybe a thank you for flying Andy and Zoey home." He wrinkled his nose and took a backward step toward the door.

I placed my hands on my hips. "You have no idea what roses mean, do you?" I frowned.

What did I want Blake to know? *He's made a mess of my life.* What message should Jim share with him? *I'm done.* I grabbed the flower from Jim's hands, being mindful of the thorns, and dropped it on the floor. I lifted my foot to stomp it to pieces but stopped.

A new word pounded in my head. *Forgive.*

I took a deep breath, gasped, let it out slowly, and bent to pick up the rose. I straightened and stared at the lovely petals, brought the flower to my nose, and whispered, "Tell him that I placed the rose in a vase and said thank you." I opened the front door to allow my captive to go free. "Time for me to leave for the office." I didn't look at Jim when he stepped outside, and he left without saying a word.

~

At 8:20, I arrived at our office suite but wasn't concerned. After all, Jim's delivery from Blake made me late. But no need to worry. Blake wasn't in his office.

I sat at my desk and turned on my computer. Another rose? *I get it. Time to forgive. I do love him.* My love wasn't the kind I could turn on and off like a light switch. But he betrayed my trust and ripped my heart out. I bent over and held myself. This turmoil inside must stop. If this was his way of wanting another chance, I couldn't take him back. This chaos between us could last a lifetime.

Muffled voices in the hallway caused me to straighten. I didn't want someone to walk in and see me buckled over. I removed the two printed copies of my resignation letter from the folder I'd brought from home. I took them to the first-floor reception desk to use the automatic date stamp. Miranda was off for the holidays and wouldn't see the letter until late next week. I didn't want any question concerning the correct start date of my two-week notice. In addition to the dated letter, I wanted backup proof. I placed one letter on Miranda's desk and the other on Blake's.

No sign of Blake by 9:00. Maybe he decided to take the day off to spend time with Andy. That sounded perfect to me.

Allison strolled in thirty minutes later. "Good. You're here. Where's Dad?"

"I don't know where he is." *I don't care. That's not true, I care too much.* "I haven't seen him this morning."

She looked out our office suite door and checked both directions of the hallway. She stepped back inside. "Jim told me about the roses he brought you. He said they were the two-tone ones with dark pink and light orange?" She sat in the chair across from my desk.

I nodded. "Salmon color. Why your dad still gives them to me, I have no idea." I glanced toward his open office door. "But one thing I know. I'm done. My resignation letter is on his desk. I can't stay here and be his assistant when he plans to marry that woman." My chin trembled. "I love your dad. But I can only take so much. I'm not a saint."

"Yes. You are." Her expression changed to a sneer. "But Eliza. What could he possibly see in her? When did he tell you about their engagement?"

"Before I drove away." I covered my mouth with my hand and mumbled, "Merry Christmas, Keedryn. I'm marrying Eliza."

Allison reached across my desk and touched my other hand. "Could we step into the conference room in case he comes in while I'm here? I don't want to be overheard."

I stood and led the way. We closed the door, sat next to one another at the table, and faced the windows.

Allison raised her hands and brought them back down. "I don't understand what's happened. I know there's a new policy. Dad seemed to be okay to wait for you to be sure you were ready to commit to a long-term relationship. But last night he told us he planned to marry Eliza." She pressed her lips together into a slight frown.

I listened to her ramble. I was at a loss for words anyway.

"I didn't give him a chance to say anything else. I glared at Jim and said, 'Getting late. Let's go. I have a busy day tomorrow.'" She bounced her heel up and down on the floor. "And Andy said, 'Sis, I think Zoey would be more comfortable to stay at your place. Big houses give her the creeps. May we spend our time in Nashville with you?' We all left at the same time without saying anything else to Dad or Eliza." Her eyes got big. "Andy spent less than an hour with him."

"Must have been hard on both Andy and your dad." I shook my head. "What a mess this is. Maybe we don't understand what's going on in your dad's head right now, but he needs time with Andy. I hope you'll try to make that happen. A shame if Andy and Zoey leave without spending quality time with Blake."

"I agree. I'll do my best. But I won't include his fiancée." She crossed her arms.

"Tell me about the rose. I know the color meaning and the significance of giving one." I shrugged. "But why do you think he sent me one the day after his engagement to Eliza?"

"That's the main reason I came to see you. Jim said you questioned him." She waved her hand. "Jim has no idea the significance of this rose." She gazed out the window and appeared wistful. "They were Mom's favorites. Dad bought several bushes for her. He gave her one flower at a time like he has with you." She looked at me again and grinned. "That he still gave you one today means you are his one-and-only, and I couldn't be happier."

"Doesn't it bother you that your dad gives me the same rose he gave your mother to convey his love for her?"

"I've seen such an amazing change in Dad these past two months due to your being a part of his life." She shook her head and smiled. "I don't wish to ever see him return to his grumpiness and grief-stricken state." Allison touched my arm. "Does it bother you?"

"No. I've been pleased to know that after five years he wanted to share such a personal part of himself with me."

I slumped back into my chair. "But he told me last night, 'It's too late.'" I leaned forward and placed my elbow on the table and propped my cheek on my fist. "I must agree with him. I don't think what's happened can be repaired."

Allison placed her hand in front of me on the conference table. "He doesn't love Eliza." She tapped her hand on the table. "He loves you. He'd give these roses to Mom and say things like, 'You're the light of my life.' Or, 'I love you just because.' He's a romantic guy." She stared toward the corner of the room. "He told me recently, Mom stopped accepting these gifts. In her depression, she wouldn't talk to him about it. And he knew for sure then something was dreadfully wrong."

I placed my hand on top of Allison's.

She turned her head back toward me. "What made saying yes to Dad's proposal difficult for you? I think he's made great progress in his return to the Lord. You said you weren't ready to commit and wanted to pray. I understand that. I do. But what held you back?"

I peered at our hands. "For the past three and a half years, I've learned to rely on God and God alone. My life is fixed on Him. If Blake doesn't fully walk with the Lord, we'll be divided. We won't share that common bond. I'm concerned I'll live my life to please my husband first and not be fully devoted to God. That frightens me." I bit my lip. "I wanted the two of us committed to serve Him together—to pray together and be in harmony with the Lord."

"Have you told him this?"

"Wes tried to tell him Friday."

"Wes?"

I told Allison that Wes came into our office and preached to Blake. I softened what I said. I didn't want to cause further division between her and Blake. I also told her about his comment regarding Eliza not having ulterior motives.

Allison grabbed her chair's armrests. "Without ulterior motives? All that woman wants is his money." She stood and glared at me. "Are you going to sit by and let him marry her?"

"Me?" I stood, too, forcing Allison to back up. "This is in God's hands. Your dad needs Him more than he needs me." I took a couple of steps toward the door, which was ajar. Before I could say anything, Blake entered and closed the door behind him.

Allison and I gaped at him with wide eyes.

She took a step closer. "How long have you been standing there?"

He rubbed his hand over his chin and mouth. "A few minutes."

Allison pinched her eyebrows together. "Are you going to marry Eliza? Or is this a ploy to get BCH off your back?"

This was a family discussion. Not my family. I stared at the floor and hurried toward the door.

Blake gently touched my arm when I passed him. "I'd like us to talk again." He stepped in front of me, and I peered up at him. "Eliza set a date of January 12."

Allison grabbed Blake's arm. "Are you crazy? Two weeks?"

Blake's mouth twisted. He turned to look at Allison. "I wanted to talk this through with K. See if there's any chance for us before I make the biggest mistake of my life. I've made a major mess of things." He turned toward me. "But after what I overheard, I doubt you want anything to do with me."

He reopened the door and trudged to his office. Allison grabbed her purse and followed him. His closed door didn't stop her.

Thankful to be alone, I moved to the window and gazed at the street below. Blake used my nickname again—K, a name he liked to call me during tender moments. But this didn't feel like a tender moment to me. Hard to believe he wanted to know if we could fix things between us. I didn't want to talk to him or see him. I didn't want anything to do with him.

What now? What do I do about Nicki's Papa? Forgive. I know.

I returned to my desk. With this being Christmas week, not many tasks awaited me. Time to investigate before lunch. I didn't know why I hadn't researched before now. Allison's comments concerning her mom stirred up that inquisitive place in me. Blake was convinced Cheryl's death was not an accident. I'd been curious as to what happened that evening.

Allison came out of Blake's office and closed his door behind her. "I know he's hurt you deeply."

"He has hurt me." I folded my hands together on top of my desk. "But I've hurt him too. I guess we need to forgive each other and see where that leads."

"He's in there sulking." She plopped on the chair across from my desk. "Like I said earlier, you are his one-and-only. He loves you."

"I know he does. He thinks if he marries Eliza, I'll marry Wes. He wants what's best for me. But Wes isn't my best." I rested my elbows on my desk and cupped my cheeks in my hands.

"He read your resignation letter while I was in there. He looked defeated." Allison stood. "I need to leave. Know I'm here for you."

After she left, I brought up Google on my computer. It didn't take long to find a short blurb dealing with the accident that occurred on March 6, almost six years earlier. I confirmed the time of day was 5:45 p.m.—sunset. The article didn't give an exact location but did confirm Cheryl was traveling east on Otter Creek Road toward Franklin Pike, which meant she was leaving Radnor Lake. I gathered new information as well. A misty rain fell that afternoon and into the early evening. The article stated Cheryl apparently lost control on the curvy, wet road. She was driving too fast and not wearing a seatbelt.

I rarely went out during my lunch hour unless I was joining someone else. I usually sat in one of the small meeting rooms or the company break room to eat a lunch I packed. Today, I needed to get away to think and pray. My stomach still churned, my chest hurt, and I developed a throbbing headache. I hopped into my car and drove to Radnor Lake, which was five miles away.

Traveling west on Otter Creek Road, I soon came to the parking area. Jenny and Carl brought me out here a couple of times but not on a chilly day like today. I parked and slid out of my car to walk a bit. The temperature was colder than on Christmas Day— dropped to the thirties. Too cold for me without my heavier coat. I got back into my car and opened the

Bible stored in my glove compartment.

I turned to the book of Hosea—the book I sensed the Lord wanted me to read when He said, "Forgive." A small book of fourteen chapters, I read the first three and skimmed the rest. The Lord showed me what He wanted me to do. I hoped things hadn't gone awry between Blake and Eliza as they did in Hosea's story. But I was ready to love, accept, and forgive as Hosea did, and as God continues to do with me daily.

I peeked at my watch and shrieked. Having been gone more than an hour and a half, I needed to hurry to get back to the office. I pulled out my cell to send Blake a text. *No service?* I left the parking area and drove a quarter of a mile before I realized my seat belt wasn't buckled. When I grabbed the belt, I swerved slightly to the right. I hit my brakes but continued to swerve. I was thankful when I came to a complete stop, but I couldn't shake the thought of what had happened. *What if this same scenario played itself out with Cheryl?*

Eighteen

I zipped into our office suite and saw Blake's door ajar. He sat at his desk. I tapped on the door and raced inside. Gone an hour longer than usual.

"Sorry." I shoved my hands into my jacket pockets. "I took a drive and lost track of time."

He clasped his hands together on his desk and stared at me. "I was worried about you." He sounded agitated. "You usually tell me when you think your lunch will run long. Nothing was on your calendar."

"I tried to text you when I saw the time, but there wasn't any cell service."

"Hard to believe." He scowled. "Where did you go?"

I let out a long breath. "I drove to Radnor Lake. To think."

He stood and came to the front of his desk. "Of all places, K. Why there?"

"I hoped to find clarity as to what the Lord was asking of me. I did." I peered into his eyes. "Also, something happened I need to share with you. Can we meet after work?" I wanted to give Blake a glimmer of hope and for him to see God's love through me.

He shook his head. "Pointless." He crossed his

arms.

Sounded final. I wanted to shake him. He was playing with my heart again.

"But Jim delivered a rose from you this morning." I got as close to him as I could without touching him. "A 'my one-and-only' gift. If I've learned anything about you, I know you communicate your feelings through roses." He stood like a stone statue. "What's going on inside of you? Talk to me." I turned away from him. I didn't want him to see me fall apart. My body shook. I wanted to run out the door and not look back. He was impossible.

"I've messed up too much. I'm not the man you want or need." He spoke with compassion. Something I hadn't heard from his lips for several days. "I'm not good enough or deserving enough to have you as my wife. I failed Cheryl. I'll fail you too."

I turned to face him and sniffled. "When Allison was here you said you wanted to talk to me. To see if we can fix this. Have you changed your mind already? Or do you still want to talk?"

He told me that he was invited to Allison's that evening for dinner and to visit with Andy. "Are you available tomorrow evening?"

I nodded and closed my eyes for a moment. "Should we meet at Jenny's? I'm sure she'd let us use the bonus room again."

"Fine. But I don't think you understand. I'm not the man to lead you in your spiritual walk. I'd be a constant disappointment to you."

Part of me wanted to say, yeah, I think you're right. Let's forget everything. But that wasn't a part of God's plan today. I needed to trust Him. We confirmed we'd meet at Jenny's the following evening, a decision that I hoped wouldn't destroy me.

Late in the afternoon I remembered Nicki's envelope. Blake was getting ready to leave for the day.

I caught him on his way out the door. "I have something for you. Nicki will be disappointed if you don't get this today. She drew you several pictures for your Christmas present from her." I grabbed her gift, moved to the front of my desk, and handed Blake the sealed envelope. "Papa Blake" was written across the front.

He took out the paper and held the drawings as if they were a priceless treasure. After he read what she'd written, he returned the paper to me. She'd drawn a picture of a man and a little girl holding hands and labeled the picture, "Me and Papa Blake after Nana's wedding."

She also drew a picture of Jesus labeled, "I love you and forgive you."

I let out a deep breath, flipped the paper over, and read the back. "Did you read what she wrote here?"

Blake took the drawings from me and read aloud. "I missed you at my birthday party and Christmas. I wanted to see you again. You are my Papa. Jesus told me that He loves you." He paused. "Nana loves you too," he whispered. "Can I be your flower girl at Nana's wedding?" He gave a slight chuckle. "She keeps saying, 'Nana's wedding.'"

I kept my voice soft and low. "She's including you too. She understands we need to be married for you to be her papa." I pointed to the words he'd read. "Please look at this again. There's a comma before 'Jesus told me' and a period after. She meant to say, 'Jesus told me that you are my papa. He loves you.'"

"Do you think Tauni's statement was true?" His face tightened, and he cocked his head. "Nicki has a spiritual gift?"

I shrugged. "Something we can explore tomorrow evening."

His jaw quivered. He gazed deep into my eyes. "But I've hurt you plenty. How can you forgive me?"

"Are you able to forgive me?" I pulled a stray thread off the collar of his shirt. "I know I've hurt you too." I peered into his blue eyes.

He reached over to caress my cheek.

I took a sideways step. His finger barely brushed my face. "I plan to resign. But if we get caught being chummy, you could face early retirement."

"Tomorrow evening then." With a hint of a smile, he took a step back and held the drawings to his chest. "Tell Nicki I'll keep this in a special place."

We gave each other a wave and said good night.

The Lord used Nicki and her drawings. Appeared they softened Blake's heart. I closed my eyes and prayed.

~

On my way home, I stopped at Montel's to order a bouquet. Such a beautiful shop. The smell of fresh-cut flowers drifted past my nose. The florist greeted me and guided me to a lovely display of deep red roses. I planned to take a huge step of faith.

She waggled her eyebrows and told me dark reds declare you're ready for a long-term commitment and make a bold statement of love. She also suggested I purchase twenty-one deep reds because the number twenty-one also meant commitment.

Too expensive on my salary, but I caved and told her that I'd pick them up the following afternoon to save a $20.00 delivery fee.

Blake took Thursday off and sent a text to confirm we still planned to meet at Jenny's. He offered to bring dinner. In my return text, I told him that Jenny had it covered. I found things to keep me busy during the morning and met Tauni for lunch since we couldn't meet the day before as we originally planned. We chatted about Blake and Eliza's engagement, how I was holding up, and how we each spent Christmas Day. She also shared that she and Mitch were still a couple.

Because things could go either way between Blake and me, I tried to keep things positive but not say too much. I let her do most of the talking, and she made me laugh a couple of times, a blessing I needed.

I took the afternoon off and made a couple of stops on my way home. The main stop was the florist.

~

I arrived at Jenny's at 5:30. Blake planned to be there at 6:00. I wanted to get the flowers inside and hidden before he arrived.

Jenny greeted me at the door. "Are those for me?" She stuck her nose in the middle of the bouquet.

"They're for Blake."

"Why did you buy roses for Blake?" She rubbed her bottom lip.

"Because my daughter told me to."

She jerked her head back. "Me? When?"

"When you told me Blake may need me to commit to him to understand how the Lord forgives, accepts, and loves him too."

Jenny rose on her tiptoes and clapped her hands.

"I'm excited." Her shoulders sagged, and she seemed serious. "But couldn't you have bought one? Still means commitment."

While we strolled down the hallway toward the living room, I explained how twenty-one roses also signify, I'm committed to you. "If he doesn't understand God's and my love with these, I don't know what will convince him." I scanned the living room. "Where's Nicki?"

"She and Carl rushed to the store. We have a meatloaf in the oven, and I ran out of ketchup." She breathed in the scent of the flowers. "Not fancy for a rich guy, but all I could come up with on short notice."

"Please don't be upset with me if I don't eat much. I'm rather nervous concerning this conversation." I slid my purse off my shoulder and held the vase with one hand. "He's wounded my heart more than once."

The garage door moaned, alerting us Carl and Nicki had returned. "I'll put these in the bedroom upstairs, out of sight, and fetch them at the right moment." I started up the stairs.

Jenny followed me with her eyes. "Are you concerned he may say no?"

I stopped halfway up. "Yes. He told me, 'It's over.' He was touched by Nicki's drawings, though." I stared ahead. "I think that meant more than he let on." I continued my climb upstairs, hid the bouquet, and returned in time to see Nicki barge through the door with a grocery bag.

She flung the bag on the kitchen counter and ran toward me. "I'm happy to see you." She hugged my legs. "Where's my Papa Blake?"

"He'll be here soon, sweetie. He's on his way to

see you."

"Yay." She jumped up and down. "Did he like my gift?"

"You may ask him when he gets here."

She danced all over the house like a ballerina, fluttering here and there.

When the doorbell rang, Nicki sprinted down the hallway to the front door. "Papa Blake is finally here." Jenny and I followed.

My heart did a summersault when he stepped through the front door. *I do love him. But can this be repaired? He's still broken and now I'm broken too.*

When Blake picked up Nicki, she wrapped her arms around his neck and said, "I love you. I'm happy you came to see me."

My eyes locked onto Blake's. I fought tears. His eyes glistened too. The Spirit of God ran through my granddaughter's veins. She had a gift for bringing people together. God used her at that moment to let me know all things were working together for His good. He was still in control.

"What's in the box, Papa?"

"What box are you talking about little girl?"

She giggled. "The one you put on the floor when you picked me up. Is that for me?"

"That present is for your Nana." He looked at me and back at Nicki. "But your gift will arrive before I leave tonight. How does that sound?"

"Not a living gift, is it?" Jenny sounded stern.

"As a matter of fact, yes. But he won't be staying here if that's why you're concerned."

"Good. All we need is a pony in the backyard."

Nicki leaned her head back and laughed. "Yay. A

pony." She wriggled out of Blake's arms. "Did you like my drawings?"

"I loved your drawings." He nodded. "I put it where I'll see it every day. On my refrigerator."

"Nicki. Please go wash up, and let Nana talk to Papa Blake." I dipped my head and squeezed my eyes shut. "Oh, goodness. Now she has me saying it."

When I glanced up, he gave me a slight grin.

Carl entered the hallway, welcomed Blake, and shook his hand. While Carl carried Blake's coat upstairs along with the wrapped gift, Jenny called us to the dining room. Nicki sat next to Blake on one side of the table. Jenny, Carl, and I sat across from them. A great seat for watching Blake and Nicki interact.

After Carl prayed, Nicki patted Blake's hand. "When will my gift get here?"

"Honey." Jenny didn't give Blake time to answer. "Eat your dinner and let Blake eat his."

"But Mama. I'm excited."

I leaned forward. "Nicki, you're too funny."

Blake winked at her and she beamed.

Carl and Jenny did most of the talking when Nicki wasn't interrupting them. We finished dinner, and Jenny and I stood to clear the table. Minutes later the doorbell rang.

Nicki sprinted to the front door. "My present. My present. My present is here." She sang the words while she ran.

Blake and Carl both got up and darted down the hallway to join her, and I followed. Nicki opened the door and stared for a moment before she jumped up and down and said, "Scotty's here."

Scotty Nelson? The hallway wasn't well lit, but I

was sure this man, holding a guitar case, at the door was the real Scotty.

Blake introduced him to Carl, Jenny, and me. I asked Blake how they knew each other. Before he could respond, Nicki whisked Scotty down the hall and into the living room. Carl and Jenny followed.

Eyes aglow, Blake leaned toward me. "My uncle was in the music business. That's where he made his fortune. Part of his estate assists young people getting started in both country and Christian music. I make those disbursement decisions now that he's gone. Scotty's recommended candidates, so we've met together a few times."

I tapped my finger against my lower lip and pointed it at him. "So many things I don't know about you."

He looked at the floor. "So many things I'd like to share with you." He glanced up. "And learn about you too."

A ray of hope. His comment encouraged me to move forward and give him the flowers. But I also knew this could be my last opportunity for him to see God's love through me. I didn't want to mess this up.

"Let's not miss the concert." I wanted to offer him my hand but decided against it. "I think he's finished tuning his guitar. I doubt he'll stay long, and then we can talk."

Nicki yelled down the hallway to us. "Nana. Papa. Come quick. Scotty's going to sing to me."

We rushed down the hallway and into the living room. Scotty sang two songs from his new CD. He wished Nicki a belated happy birthday and all of us a Merry Christmas before he packed up.

After he left, Nicki ran over to Blake. "I love you."

He squatted and opened his arms.

She moved into his embrace and nuzzled close. "Did you understand what I wrote on the back of my drawings?"

He released his hold, and excitement filled his voice. "Tell me again."

"Jesus told me you're my Papa." She poked him in the chest with her finger. "That means you must marry my Nana. I can't call you that no more if you're not my Papa."

"I think I understand." His eyes danced and he hugged Nicki again.

She plopped herself onto his left knee. He lost his balance and sprawled on the floor. Nicki landed next to him, got up on her knees, and laughed for several seconds before she scrambled to her feet.

My eyes glistened to see the love that flowed between the two of them. Like they'd been a part of each other's lives since she was born. She reached out and offered her hand to Blake to help him up. Such a big grin on her face.

Carl placed his arm across Jenny's shoulder. They smiled at their daughter and one another.

After a few moments of Nicki pulling on Blake's hand, him trying to sit up, and falling back down to her delight, Blake rose to his knees and stood. We laughed at their antics.

Jenny took a step toward Nicki and told her if she wanted a bedtime story, she needed to get her bath. She whined and pouted on her way to her room to find her pajamas.

Blake climbed the stairs to the bonus room, and I

followed. He glanced back at me and said, "She's amazing. I see much of you in her."

When we got to the top of the stairs, I slipped in front of him and we stood face-to-face. "Me?"

"She oozes kindness, acceptance, and an over-the-top kind of love for Jesus. She's a little Keedryn."

"You forgot a couple of things. She's forgiving too. She didn't hold a grudge against you because your birthday gift was late. She also thinks the world of you and loves you beyond comprehension." I whispered, "You're correct. She's a little me."

Blake sat in a chair across from the couch. "I meant what I said yesterday."

I turned away and closed my eyes. *This is too hard.* I looked back at Blake and took a seat on the sofa. "When you said, getting together tonight was pointless?"

He leaned toward me. "That was me being foolish. I meant when I said, 'I've made a mess of things.'"

"Agreed."

He frowned and leaned back. "How can you forgive me?" He rubbed the back of his neck. "I've been hateful and cruel to you."

I wanted to invite him to join me on the couch. We currently sat six feet away from one another, an example of the disconnect between us.

"Have you ever read the book of Hosea?"

He nodded and stared at the wall above my head. "Although the temptation has been strong, the Lord always gives me a way of escape." He peered at me. "Eliza is relentless. You must pray for me constantly." He leaned forward, placed his hands on his knees, and spoke just above a whisper. "Allison told me last night about the extra time you've spent in prayer. Faithful to seek the Lord for us since this policy fiasco started. I'm not worth the trouble."

"None of us are. I read from the book of Hosea while I was at Radnor Lake yesterday. God's people did horrible things—adultery, idol worship, and murder, but the Lord received them back. He pursued them in love—forgave and accepted them." I closed my eyes for a moment and prayed for God to move in Blake's heart. "God hasn't changed. He still takes us back when we mess up. How can I not do the same?"

I shared a few details of my experience at Radnor Lake, and how I'd nearly lost control of my car. I emphasized the likelihood Cheryl's accident could have happened in a similar way.

Blake shook his head. "There were signs of depression. Comments under her breath."

"But is there a possibility, during the two or three hours from the time she left the house until the accident, she may have prayed and decided you were correct? That she needed help?"

He clasped his hands together and placed them in his lap. "Our family is and has always been seatbelt freaks. We buckle up 100-percent of the time. But she wasn't wearing hers at the time of the accident."

My arms tingled and I remembered my seatbelt. I told Blake how I'd unbuckled it to go for a walk and decided the weather was too chilly. I got back in my car, read my Bible, and prayed. "After I drove off, I realized my belt wasn't hooked. I tried to buckle up. That's when I nearly drove off the road. If the roads were wet and slippery, getting dark, her situation may have been similar."

"She was also driving too fast."

"Perhaps in a moment of panic she hit the gas when she tried to break."

He stared at the floor.

"I believe God will give you peace regarding whatever happened if you'll trust Him and forgive yourself." I stood. "I'll be right back."

I zipped into the bedroom and brought out the bouquet. I placed the vase on the coffee table next to the package Blake brought and looked at him with tears in my eyes. "These are for you." I returned to the sofa.

Without moving, he gazed at the roses for a couple of minutes. *Will he again tell me, it's too late?*

Blake stood, shuffled over to where I sat, and knelt to the right of me. He put his head on the couch and wept. He asked the Lord for forgiveness.

I placed my hand over my mouth to muffle my cries and rocked back and forth.

No doubt in my mind. I sensed the Lord moved deeply in Blake. I prayed quietly along with him and gave him the space and time he needed.

After nearly ten minutes, Blake pulled away from the sofa, took the package from the coffee table, and offered the gift to me. "This is you."

"You mean this is for me?" I straightened.

"This *is* you. How would you describe this package?"

I chuckled. "The bottle of Jack Daniels." A few months earlier, Blake sent me out to buy a bottle of Jack Daniels for a retiree. He didn't specify whiskey, so I bought barbeque sauce. He in return brought me a lovely wrapped present with only a handwritten note inside.

"This is a beautifully wrapped gift. Extremely lovely on the outside." I shook the box. "Heavier than the one you brought me with a piece of paper inside. Is there a rock in here?"

"Open it." He moved from the floor to take his place next to me on the sofa.

I carefully unwrapped the blue and white striped package. My hands trembled. "Oh." I tipped my head back for a moment and closed my eyes. "Beautiful on the inside too." Kintsugi—the Japanese art of repairing broken pottery with gold. He remembered something I'd shared with him three months earlier during our difficult days. I looked deep into his eyes. "A gift I will treasure forever."

There. The twinkle he worked hard to disguise this past week. His eyes crinkled, and his smile deepened.

He took the bowl in his hands and gazed into my eyes. "This is you. After all the pain and heartache, you're more beautiful to me than before. Your Christ-like love, which I don't deserve, makes you more valuable and precious than I ever imagined. I love you with almost everything in me."

My heart raced. I moved my hand to my chest. "Almost?" I whispered.

"I believe tonight, I gave God my everything."

Nineteen

On Friday morning, I arrived at the office with a new song in my heart. Blake fell in love with the Lord all over again. I thought back to the time three months earlier when I'd first asked the Lord to release me from BCH. Now, I was thankful I stayed and could share in this blessing.

Blake planned to take most of the day off but said he'd stop by early for a few minutes.

He strode past me with a bounce in his step when he arrived at 8:15.

I followed him into his office, and we stood in front of his desk. I told him that in addition to informing Miranda, I'd emailed my resignation to Chad that morning and would tell Tauni and Beth too.

"What about Wes?" Blake moved to the other side of his desk, sat, and logged into his computer.

"He's out of the office this week. I didn't want to bother him."

He turned to face me and tapped a pen repeatedly on top of a file folder opened on his desk. "I need to apologize to him." He rubbed his hand across his mouth. "Schedule a time Monday morning for me to meet with Wes here in my office."

On Blake's way out, at 9:00, he asked me to pray. His major errand was Eliza's house to break off their engagement. She expected Blake to buy her a diamond today, not end their relationship. He was concerned with her reaction and said she sometimes gets nasty. I bit my tongue. No need to tell me something I knew. *Poor Eliza.* I did feel a tiny bit sorry for her.

He also asked me to meet him at Allison's at 1:00 p.m. She expected him, but he wanted my arrival to be a surprise.

I took the stairs down to the second floor to visit Tauni and told her that I'd resigned. Tears puddled in her eyes. She thanked me for being a good friend, perhaps her best. We talked about continuing our weekly time together and how she would be a viable candidate to take my place as Blake's executive assistant.

Tauni shook her head. "I could never be you." She stuck out her lower lip.

I reached down and hugged her. "You better not be me," I whispered. "He can be your boss, but I won't share him in any other way."

She pulled away and straightened. "What? You mean?" Her eyes widened. "The two of you?"

I raised my index finger to my mouth to quiet her. "Seems that way. Don't tell anyone yet. He's breaking off his engagement with Eliza now."

"He needs lots of prayer to get out of there alive." She bowed her head and appeared to pray. When she finished, she gave me a thumbs up. "That should do it."

I laughed. "He asked me to pray for him when he left. Now he's received double prayer power."

"No ring?" She glanced at my left hand.

"He hasn't officially proposed, but I think he will soon. I didn't plan to tell anyone, but I blabbed to you in a weak moment."

"Your secret's safe. Thanks for confiding in me. I'm happy for you both." Her gaze darted to the corner of the room. "But Blake won't want me as his assistant. I've messed up too many times." She looked at me and down at her lap. "He must think I'm a bimbo."

"Not at all. You inspired him. He recently said, if God can change Tauni's heart, there may be hope for me too."

She lifted her head and her eyes sparkled.

I beamed and leaned toward her. "His hope came last night."

"He prayed last night like I did at the women's conference in October?"

I nodded.

We talked a few more minutes before I returned to my office to call Beth who'd taken the week off to spend time with her family. I told her that I'd given my two-week's notice. I didn't have time to share any details. Her youngest grandchild insisted she play hide and seek.

Blake called at 10:00. "Eliza took the news hard. She didn't cry much, but she screamed a lot and threw a few things."

"I hope you're okay." I lowered my voice. "I think something's going down here. Walt was in the hallway a couple of minutes ago. Miranda was yelling, but I thought she was off through next week."

"Maybe the board's reviewing the new policy again and called her in. I'll call Chad. Don't worry. I'll let you know what's going on. See you at 1:00?"

"Why do you want me there?"

"I think you'll enjoy my family's response when I tell them that I broke off my engagement with Eliza. Also, I plan to tell them what happened to me last night and apologize for being a goofus of a dad."

I chuckled. "Sounds like one of Allison's names for Andy." I paused. "Lance is here too. And Chad. And that fancy dressed lawyer I see from time to time, Mr. Samuels."

"Samuels is there?" He sighed. "I'll ask Chad about him too."

We ended our call, and I finalized a letter Blake wanted finished before I left for the day.

A few minutes later, Chad entered our suite looking for Blake. I told him that Blake planned to call him soon but took the rest of the day off. Chad requested a meeting with Blake and me at 2:30, if possible, to discuss an important matter.

I left the office at 11:30 and rushed home to grab a bite to eat and relax a bit before I drove to Allison's.

When I arrived at Allison's at 1:00, Blake's car was parked in front of the house.

Zoey answered the door. "Finally. I'm happy to see you," she whispered. "But Blake's here too."

"I saw his car." I followed Zoey through the foyer, past the dining room and into the living room which joined an empty open kitchen/eating area. "Where is everyone?"

"They're in Allison's bedroom having a family conference. She pointed to a room behind the fireplace. You can join me on the sofa or sit on the loveseat, and we'll wait together."

I sat in the middle of the sofa which was positioned

in front of four windows. Zoey was next to me on my left. I asked her how she felt and what fun things they'd done since their arrival in Nashville. She mentioned the Grand Ole Opry and shopping.

The bedroom door squeaked open, and Allison appeared with a paper notebook in her hand. "Keedryn. I wasn't expecting you. I'm happy you're here but surprised." She shuffled back a couple of steps. "Dad's here too." Worry lines formed across her forehead. "Maybe you should come back another time. We're having a family discussion in my room."

"I'm fine, Allison. You finish up while I visit with Zoey."

Blake and Andy followed her out. Blake stood next to the fireplace, and Andy sat on the floor in front of Zoey.

Blake focused on Allison. "Let's talk out here. Keedryn and Zoey should be included in our conversation."

Allison frowned and settled in on the loveseat. "What's going on here, Dad? I love Keedryn, and I'm happy to see her, but why bring her in on something this sensitive regarding our family?"

I stood. "Maybe I shouldn't be here."

Blake moved to my side and touched my arm. "Yes. You should." He glanced around the room at his family gathered together. "I asked Keedryn to join us. I need to tell you all that earlier today I broke off my engagement with Eliza."

I expected cheers but saw blank expressions except for a grin on Zoey's face. What was going on? My chest felt heavy. Something was wrong. What took place in Allison's room?

Allison stood. "I don't understand why you asked her to marry you in the first place. You of all people should have known what she was capable of."

My eyes darted back and forth between Blake and Allison. *What did Eliza do?*

Blake sat on my right and held my hand. "I never planned to marry Eliza. She pestered me about getting engaged. I thought if I made it official, you and Wes would get together, and I would tell Eliza the wedding was off." He brushed his thumb over mine. "I never expected her to insist on a wedding date in January. I thought I had several months to see what happened between you and Wes."

Blake looked at Allison. "Give Keedryn the journal so she can read aloud what we read." He spoke with compassion.

She tapped her fingernails against the cover of the notebook. "Are you sure you want her to know this? I don't want to scare her away."

"She'll be fine. She and Zoey need to know."

I stepped over to where Allison sat, took the journal from her outstretched arms, and peered at Blake. "What am I reading?"

He moved over in front of the fireplace again and motioned for me to stand next to him. "This was Cheryl's journal beginning four months before she died. We're reading an entry from two months later, so two months before her accident."

My hands shook. I was asked to read something personal and possibly emotional. I took a deep breath. I read an entry dated January 8: "I'm broken. Eliza's been telling me if I don't come out of this hole, I will lose Blake forever. I've not been a good wife. I hate feeling like this. Ugly. Unloved. Which until now was stupid because he's given me no reason to feel that way. He's always spoken encouraging words and told me that he loves me. I try to smile and act happy. But something's wrong. Eliza said she thinks he's been unfaithful to me. She's told me this for a couple of months. Today what she told me left me numb. I've lost him to her."

I stopped reading. My heart broke for a woman whom I'd never met. I glanced up from the journal and scanned the room. Blake nudged me to continue.

"Eliza wept when she confessed to me today. Blake made a move on her, and in her weakness, she gave in to his advances. She apologized over and over. I forgave her. But I can't forgive Blake. I didn't think he'd betray me. I don't know what I'm going to do."

I looked from Blake to Allison to Andy, but they all stared at the floor. Andy picked at the carpet.

This can't be true. "Despicable lies." I spoke from my heart.

Allison shuffled over and hugged me. "I admire your faith in Dad. I believe Eliza's accusations to be false because I witnessed his love for Mom, and because I know Eliza and what she's capable of." She returned to the loveseat.

Blake whispered in my ear. "I know you haven't asked. But for the record, you're correct. I did not have an affair with that woman. There was no physical contact or emotional connection between us." He gazed into my eyes. "I was never unfaithful to Cheryl."

"I believe you," I whispered.

Poor Cheryl. Eliza lied and convinced her that she wasn't a good wife and that Blake had been unfaithful.

Deception. Evil. I returned to the sofa next to Zoey, thumbed through the journal, and peered at Allison. "The entries must be difficult to read. How many journals are there? And how many have you read?"

"I've skimmed several. Her older journals are filled with family and love. I didn't find any signs of depression until the September before she died. What we read today was the most emotional. There's been moodiness before this but not the hopelessness."

I stood to return the journal to Allison and flipped to the back. I noticed the date on the final entry. February 13. Three weeks before Cheryl's accident. "Is there another one after February 13?" I returned to the sofa.

Blake nodded. "I believe so. I seem to remember her writing on into March. I'll keep searching."

The family discussed the troubling information from the journal for several minutes. Allison agreed to let them know if she came across other entries that might shed light on how Cheryl suffered.

Blake hung his head. "I can't believe I became engaged to that woman." He focused on his family. "I'm sorry for putting you all through what I have these past couple of weeks with Eliza."

Blake again took a seat on my right. He asked me to share my story from Wednesday's visit to the lake. When I finished, Andy and Allison appeared relieved. They both thanked me. Blake told the family that he believed Cheryl may have been on her way home that evening. An accident like the police report stated.

He stood again and looked at each person individually. "I'm sorry Jim's at work and Tim's with his other grandparents and not able to be with us today.

But I'm thankful you are all here to be a part of my next announcement." He glanced at me, smiled, and looked again at Allison and Andy. "I rededicated my life to the Lord last night."

Allison jumped up, grabbed his neck, squealed, and smothered him in kisses. "Daddy, I'm excited. I want to hear how this happened." She raised her hands and moved back to the loveseat.

"I'm sorry I wandered far away from God since your mom's death. I hope to do better being the dad and grandpa I should have been all along. I owe a lot to the persistence of this beautiful woman here." He took a couple of steps toward me and extended his hand. He led me to the center of the room and faced me—his blue eyes glimmered.

"Keedryn, since you came into my life, I have been a torn man. You drove me crazy with all your God talk and your sweet spirit. I especially liked the way you flirted when you tried hard not to. Your spunk and feistiness have been my favorite companions these past several months. I love you more than life itself." He grinned. "Except for God. He's first."

He moved down on one knee and pulled out a ring. "Will you marry me even though you know what you're getting yourself into?"

I could see Allison out of the corner of my eye. She stood and held her hands on her chest. I gazed deep into Blake's eyes staring up at me. "I believe my coming to work for BCH was a part of God's plan for both of us." I rubbed my arms. "I fell in love with you with the touch of your hand on top of mine during a moment of turbulence on our trip to New Mexico." I bit at my lower lip. "Probably a sign from God to expect more in the future."

He frowned. "Is that a yes?"

"Yes." I giggled. "Put that ring on my finger."

He slid the ring on my hand and told me it belonged to his grandmother. A diamond and platinum solitaire over 100 years old. *Stunning.*

Zoey and Allison sprinted to my side. We hugged, laughed, and cried.

I grabbed Blake's arm. "Will you allow Andy and Zoey to stay and pay any increase in cost for their airline tickets?"

"Sure."

I looked at Zoey and Andy and clapped my hands. "Will Tuesday work for you two?"

"What? New Year's Day?" Zoey's eyes got big.

Blake made another face. "You two ladies are talking in code. What's going on?"

"They're talking about having a double ceremony on Tuesday." Andy chuckled. "Zoey and I are engaged too." He wrapped his arm around Zoey's waist. "We hoped to get married while here with family. Zoey wants a double wedding. Didn't seem like that could happen until now."

Allison squealed again. "Two weddings." She bounced on her toes. "We can do this."

Blake made a huge effort to get everyone's attention by waving his arms. "Wait a minute. Stop everything." His voice boomed throughout the room, and he pointed at me. "You. My Keedryn." He made dramatic pauses as he spoke. "Want to get married on Tuesday, January 1? Four days from now?"

I laughed at his expression and gestures. "Is that too soon for you? Do you need more time to prepare?" I peeked at my watch and back at Blake. "The time. We need to skedaddle and get to the office."

"Is it almost 2:30? Chad told me about the meeting when I called him this morning. We need to hurry." Blake shook his head. "I can't believe you don't need another six months or more to plan a wedding. I expected we'd get married next summer."

I reached up to cup his cheek in my hand. "I'm not taking any chances. God said, yes. I'm not giving you time to change your mind."

Twenty

I gave Andy and Zoey all the information they needed to get a marriage license. We agreed to meet at the County Clerk's office at 3:45 p.m. and hoped we'd have enough time because they'd close at 4:30.

Blake hurried to catch up to me on my dash to the front door.

I glanced back at Andy and Zoey before we left. "Kids, your license will cost $100. Dad's buying. We'll hurry."

Allison let out a cry and ran toward us with Andy close behind. "I need my car for an appointment. I can't get them to the County Clerk's office by 3:45."

I scrounged though my purse for my keys and tossed them to Andy. "Be careful."

"Are you sure you want to do that?" Blake whispered in my ear.

"Not like I own a Porsche. Besides, he's family." I waved goodbye to Andy and Allison.

Blake opened the door and we stepped outside. "I like the way you took charge in there. But how do you know what a marriage license costs?" He hesitated at the passenger door of his car.

"I Googled it before I left the office."

"You were pretty sure I'd propose today, weren't you?" He grinned. "But are you sure about getting married so soon?"

"I'm sure." I kissed his cheek.

Blake opened my door and darted to the driver's side. He started the car but didn't pull away from the curb. "I think we should take our time. I'm afraid you may regret making such a quick decision."

"I'm sure, Blake. Are you having second thoughts?" I peeked at the clock. "We've got to run. Chad's waiting on us."

~

On our drive to the office, Blake told me that he'd talked to Chad and learned what happened that morning. He didn't know all the details but said I'd be pleased.

We were welcomed when we arrived at Chad's office. He pointed to his round table, and Blake and I sat next to one another.

Chad took the seat to Blake's left and looked across the table at me. "I have news for you. I'm not sure how this will affect the two of you or if you'll change your mind and stay at BCH. But we terminated Miranda and Lance this morning."

I placed my right hand on my chest. "Thank you, Lord."

Blake eased back in his chair. His eyes glowed when he turned toward me. "I thought you'd be happy to hear that news."

"I understand Miranda's jealousy consuming her to the point of hatred and revenge." I shook my head and narrowed my eyes. "But what motivated Lance to join ranks with her?"

Chad cleared his throat. "Keep this confidential." He peered at Blake and reminded him of Lance's story to the executive team concerning his former company—the sexual harassment case between an executive and his assistant. "Lance was the executive and the guilty one."

Blake's jaw slackened. "Why did Miranda hire him? She should have known that."

"She hired him under the condition he'd help out in her plan to make Keedryn's life miserable. The rumors started with them."

Blake leaned forward. "That's crazy. Terminating their employment is letting them off easy." Blake reached under the table for my hand. "What will happen with the new policy?"

"The board wants to keep it. We may make revisions soon, but they felt a stricter policy was necessary. We'll also continue with the older two—our harassment policy and our relatives not working together policy if one is supervising another."

Chad studied both of us. "What's going on with you two?" He glanced at Blake. "I assumed Keedryn resigned because you were engaged to Eliza." His eyes met mine. "But you seem more relaxed with one another today."

"She did resign because of my engagement." Blake pulled my left hand to the top of the table and moved it toward Chad. "But now because of this." He smiled. "We'll soon be related."

"Congratulations." Chad stood, patted Blake on the back, and leaned to extend his hand to me. "How soon?"

Blake eyed me and peered at Chad. "We haven't

set a date. Please keep this quiet."

I opened my mouth to object, but Blake squeezed my hand, so I kept silent. The office wasn't the place to have that discussion.

Chad nodded and sat. "Walt will be relieved."

I cocked my head. "Why?"

"He said today, 'I hope Conner wises up in the next two weeks. If he marries Eliza over Keedryn, he needs to be fired. That would be an ignorant decision for someone on the executive team. We don't need a man like that at BCH.'"

"Go, Walt," I said with enthusiasm and quickly dipped my chin.

According to Chad, Walt played an important role in the investigation to terminate Miranda and Lance. He believed me when I told him that I'd never been to Blake's house. If that rumor was false, he must have thought the others were lies too. Maybe Walt wasn't such a bad guy after all.

Chad rested his elbows on the arms of his chair and brought his fingertips together. "Since you can't be Blake's executive assistant and married to him, too, I'd like you to consider staying and helping us out in HR. Jocelyn agreed to take Miranda's vacated position. She asked if you'd be interested in her former position as the HR Generalist." He leaned toward me and spoke in almost a whisper. "You'd still be able to keep an eye on Blake and make sure he stays out of trouble since your office would be down the hall."

Blake pointed to his chest. "Me? She doesn't need to keep an eye on me. I can stay out of mischief fine."

I patted his arm. "Yes, dear. We know." I looked at Chad. "I've done a little HR work in the past. May I have a week to decide?"

"Not a problem. Perhaps you can get together with Jocelyn next week to learn more about the position."

We thanked Chad for his time and support. He hugged me and shook Blake's hand. I left his office thankful that Miranda and Lance were gone.

Blake drove to the County Clerk's office and parked at 3:55 p.m.—thirty-five minutes before closing. He reached over for my hand and searched my face. "We can wait. You don't need to resign. Transfer to HR, and we can get to know one another better."

Had I manipulated him into something he wasn't ready for? I squeezed my eyes shut—my heart heavy. "But Zoey's dream is for a double wedding. I wanted to bless her by granting her wish."

I felt his palm on my cheek and opened my eyes.

"God has given us the gift of more time to grow our relationship, plus you can now stay at BCH. I love you, K, but that will be better for both of us. Gives us more time to plan too." He squeezed my hand.

Zoey will think I lied to her. She may never accept me as someone she can trust. "Zoey will be heartbroken."

"We'll find another way to bless Zoey."

I nodded and sighed. "Okay. Summer then? June or were you hoping for later?"

"You're frustrated with me. But I need to be sure that you're sure." He brought my hand to his lips and kissed my fingers. "I want to prove to you first that I can be the man God requires me to be."

I responded in a sarcastic tone. "How long do you think that will take?"

"Early April?"

"That might be doable, except Andy and Zoey won't be able to make it with a new baby."

"We could fly the rest of the family to Albuquerque and get married there."

"What about friends who'll want to share in our joy?" I pouted and crossed my arms. *Fly everyone there three months from now when Andy and Zoey are here for the next few days—doesn't make sense to me.* But I knew I wasn't going to win the argument. "You're right. Let's think this through. We don't have to decide now."

"I'm right? Should I write that down?"

"Maybe. But I don't have the heart to break this news to Zoey." I opened my car door and climbed out.

Blake met me at the back of his car and wrapped his arm across my shoulder. "I'll tell Andy and Zoey."

We walked toward the entrance of the County Clerk's office where Andy and Zoey stood waiting on us.

Blake placed his other arm across Andy's shoulder and glanced at Zoey. "We've decided to wait until spring for our wedding. You two go ahead and get your license. We'll plan a lovely ceremony for the two of you on New Year's Day." He lowered his arms, opened his wallet, and gave Andy a hundred-dollar bill.

Zoey's smile faded.

I hugged her and apologized. "Blake thinks it best if we wait a few months. Although I disagree, I've decided to honor his wishes."

She blinked away tears and looked at the sidewalk.

Andy handed me my keys, and I zipped to my car. I couldn't bear to see the disappointment on Zoey's face any longer.

Although I felt bummed, I headed to Jenny's house to share the good news regarding our engagement, prayed for Zoey along the way, and sang to my God. Such a good Father.

~

Before I got out of my car at Jenny's, I removed the ring and placed it in my pocket. I didn't want her to see it first thing—make her wonder. When I entered, she grabbed my left hand and groaned.

I pulled the ring out of my pocket and put it on my finger.

"Wow. Beautiful." She squealed and covered her mouth. "I need to hush. Nicki's taking a late nap. She wore herself out at a play date today."

Jenny prepared us both a cup of hot chocolate while I shared the specifics of how Blake proposed. "Did you set a date?"

"I suggested New Year's Day."

"You're not serious." She stopped stirring the hot chocolate—her spoon clinking against the side of the mug. "You mean four days from now?" She stared at me with wide eyes.

"Andy and Zoey are getting married that day. Zoey and I were hoping for a double ceremony."

"Are you crazy? We need time to plan." She handed me a mug, and we moved from the kitchen counter to the table and each took a seat. "Why would you consider getting married so soon?"

"I told you. Zoey has had a hard life, like mine with my aunt. I wanted to give her the desire of her heart and get married at the same time. She seemed heartbroken when she heard we weren't having a double ceremony. She didn't even speak."

Jenny squished her eyebrows together. "You'd throw away your opportunity for an amazing wedding so Zoey can have her dream? You're a saint, Mom."

"Hardly." I shook my head. "The need to move slowly with Blake was to give him more time to turn his life back over to God. When that happened, that was all I needed." I blew on my hot chocolate. "If he'd accepted my commitment to him but not found his way back, I'd extend the engagement out a year or two to allow him plenty of time to reconcile to the Lord."

"But we have a lot to do to get ready for a wedding. Don't you remember mine? Four days? We could never pull off a princess wedding that fast."

"Princess wedding?"

"Yes. Cinderella and her prince. All of BCH will want to attend. And your church people. And friends you know from my church. Can you tell I'm excited?" She clapped her hands several times. "Is Manuel going to marry you? Where are you getting married? What kind of dress will you wear? How many people do you plan to invite? Will you have a dinner reception?"

"Stop." I lifted my hand in front of her face. "We just got engaged. We have time to figure this all out because Blake said no to January first." I took a sip of my hot chocolate.

"Well at least one of you is thinking clearly." She patted my hand. "So, when? I want to help with everything. This will be fun." She hopped up and grabbed a pen and note pad from her kitchen counter. On her to-do list, she added preparations that were necessary to accomplish a wedding. In addition to the ones she'd already mentioned, she added invitations, flowers, and music.

Nicki came into the kitchen rubbing her eyes and looked up at me. "Are you spending the night here?"

"No, sweetie. I stopped by to tell your mommy that Blake and I are getting married."

Nicki crossed her arms and slightly shook her head. "Old news." She turned and trudged back toward her bedroom.

~

Blake called that evening after dinner while I journaled at the kitchen table. "There's been a change in plans. Zoey wants to wait for a double wedding. Do you mind?"

Oh, no. I closed my journal and stood. "They got their license, didn't they?"

Blake said they hadn't. "Why?"

"I told you that she wanted a double wedding. I knew this would happen." I padded to the cabinet, grabbed a cup, and opened a tea bag. "But no. You thought they'd go ahead and get married without us." I slammed the cabinet door shut a little harder than necessary. "We should have gone ahead with our plans to marry on Tuesday."

"What? Do you need me to drive over to your place so we can talk this through?" He sounded perturbed.

I filled my cup with water, placed it in the microwave and tried to tone-down my frustration. "We'll need to move up our date. The baby's due mid-March."

"Oh, I get it. Does Zoey want to get married before the baby arrives?"

"That's what I was hoping for." I grabbed my tea and plopped back into the kitchen chair. "My aunt belittled me often for being born out of wedlock. I didn't want that for our grandchild too." I rested my elbow on the table and held my forehead.

"I agree that it would be good for all of us to get married before mid-March."

"I'm sorry, I know I sound kind of down when I should be happy. But I was hoping they'd get married Tuesday." I opened my journal, grabbed my pen, and doodled roses inside.

"Maybe this will cheer you up. When I got back to Allison's, she didn't take the news well either that there were no weddings to plan in the next few days." I heard worship music playing in the background and drew a heart. "She said she loves a challenge and suggested a big celebration engagement party instead."

I leaned back. "Before Andy and Zoey fly home?"

"We were thinking Tuesday afternoon."

"I like that idea. A lot." Although I agreed that getting married on New Year's Day was not well thought out on my part, I felt disappointment that we weren't having a wedding at all. Maybe the party would be the pick-me-up I needed. "At your place?"

"Is that okay with you? We have three days to plan for the biggest event of the year."

"Oh. The engagement party will be a bigger event than our wedding?"

"No." He cleared his throat. "I forgot Tuesday starts the new year. Our wedding will be the biggest and best."

"I should hope so, especially since *you're* the one who wanted more time to plan."

Twenty-one

The next three days encompassed a whirlwind of activities. Allison and Jenny carried a full load with decorations and invitations. We couldn't have done it without their help. Blake hired a pianist and hinted Scotty Nelson might swing by to sing a couple of tunes.

On Monday morning at the office, I dropped off invitations for Tauni and Beth. I was concerned, however, to invite those on the executive team or board of directors at BCH. Someone might pass along the news to Eliza. If she showed up, there would be trouble.

Blake said he would personally invite Chad and a few others.

I called my sis, Vivian. She couldn't make it to our engagement party on such short notice. But she promised to do her best to arrange her schedule to make it to our wedding whenever we set the date.

We scheduled the party from 2:00—5:00 p.m. This would give time for guests to recover from their New Year's Eve celebrations and have plenty of time to get home early in the evening to spend time with their families. Blake planned to announce to the football fans that his theater room would be available to watch bowl games.

On Tuesday morning, Allison, Andy, Jenny, and their significant others worked alongside Blake and me to decorate Blake's house. We kept the Christmas trees and decorations in place but replaced the poinsettias with bouquets of red and white roses throughout the foyer and great room.

Andy stood nearby when I needed help moving a buffet table. "We need to move this to the right," I said, "would you help me?" He turned and walked away as if he hadn't heard me.

An hour later, Andy and Jim were laughing together just inside the kitchen. I walked up to them and said, "Good to see you two enjoying your time together."

Andy lost his smile and scooted away.

Jim turned and watched Andy stride down the hall. When Jim peered back at me, he said, "What was that about?"

I shrugged. "Guess I'm not his favorite person right now."

Odd. He welcomed me into his home in Albuquerque and seemed happy with me when he and Zoey first arrived in Nashville. What changed?

After we grabbed a light snack at noon, I pulled Jenny, Allison, and Zoey aside. "Because of everyone's help, there's not much more to do except to freshen up and change into our fancier clothes. Thank you all for helping."

I took Zoey's hand. "I'm especially excited to share this celebration with you and Andy. Today, we are celebrating your engagement as well as mine and Blake's with a double wedding soon to follow."

Zoey's eyes glistened. "I should thank all of you. You've made me feel welcomed and loved. You care about me." She sniffled. "I mean, Andy cares too. And he loves me. This is different with all of you, though. I can't explain it very well." She shook her head and looked down. "I guess what I'm trying to say is that in such a short time, you've become the family I never had."

I squeezed her hand. "And we're happy you're a part of our family."

Tears again. Such a tender heart. She raised her head. "It's hard knowing I'll leave tomorrow and won't see any of you for a long time." She stopped and wiped her hand over her eyes. "And I'm having this baby, all by myself, with no family in New Mexico. I'm scared." Her body trembled.

"Andy will be with you." I placed my arm across her shoulder.

Allison stepped closer. "I can fly out to Albuquerque if you'd like, and Dad will want to be there too."

"I'm not family yet, but if you want me there, I'll be happy to come out." I stroked Zoey's hair. "If you need me, I'm a phone call away."

Allison took a step back and wrinkled her nose. "But what's keeping you there?"

Zoey touched the base of her neck. "What?"

"What's keeping you in New Mexico?" Allison tilted her head. "This could easily be your home. Tell bumblehead you want to move to Nashville to be close to family. You want your baby to have grandparents, aunts, uncles, and cousins, too, don't you?"

Zoey's face glowed. "You're right. There's no

reason for us to stay there. During the party, I'll tell Andy it's time to move here to be near family."

~

Blake and I stood in the foyer and greeted guests. We received hugs and handshakes. Blake introduced me to his friends whom I hadn't met, and we welcomed several others from the office. These included Chad and his wife, along with Beth and her husband.

I glanced around me. Many friends made the effort to join in our celebration on short notice. *This is a special day, and I'm thrilled everyone here is a part of it.* Wes arrived alone. He shook Blake's hand and gave me a quick hug. Blake told me that he invited Wes when he'd met with him to apologize, but I never expected him to attend.

I scanned the foyer and great room and turned back to Wes. "Have you talked to Tauni?"

"She sent a text. She'll be here soon."

We all knew when Walt arrived. His loud voice echoed throughout the foyer. He grabbed Blake's hand, but when I reached out mine, he ignored it. Instead, he gathered me in an embrace that lasted a little too long in my opinion. I still wasn't sure about him.

Manuel and Susie, along with several others from my church, arrived. There were also a few from the executive team and Jocelyn, which was fine, especially if I decided to take the position in HR. There hadn't been any time to ponder that these past few days.

Blake and I, hand in hand, walked into the great room. Several round tables covered with white linen tablecloths had been set up for guests. The tables were decorated with red and white rose centerpieces. People gathered near the buffet tables and filled their plates with delicacies prepared by Blake's chef—meatballs, barbeque, crab legs, shrimp, chicken, and a taco bar. The healthier tables included various cheeses, fruits, a full salad bar, veggies, and dip. He also prepared a wide variety of desserts.

Guests enjoyed smiles, laughter, and soft piano music while they ate. A true celebration.

Tauni arrived at 2:20 and rushed over to where Blake and I stood near the buffet. "Sorry I'm late. Mitch was a booger."

"Excuse me." Blake stepped away.

Tauni huffed. "He wouldn't let me attend. He said I should be with him and not run all over town. He told me earlier that he'd planned to go watch a football game at his friend's house. But when he found out I wanted to be here with you, he stayed at my place."

"How did you get him to leave?"

She glanced around her. "I broke up with him."

"Good for you."

"I should have done that weeks ago." She rolled her eyes. "He's not God's best for me."

Blake returned to my side.

Tauni stepped back and appraised me from my head to my shoes. "You are gorgeous. I love your dress. It's the one from the date picture, right?"

I nodded. "No time to shop for another."

Tauni motioned toward Blake. "He looks okay, too, I guess." She grinned.

Blake grimaced. "If you plan to interview for Keedryn's job, you'll need to treat me with a little more respect." He pulled back his shoulders, strode to the piano, and talked with the pianist.

"I hope you have a good time. Beth, Chad, and

their spouses have a seat available at their table near the piano, and Wes is seated at the table by the fireplace." I pointed in the direction of their tables.

"Great. I'll go hang out with Beth or Wes." She paused. "Blake did know I was joking, didn't he?"

"You're good. Grab a plate and later have fun on the dance floor." I nudged her arm and pointed to the buffet.

Jenny, Carl, Allison, and Jim rearranged the furniture in the great room earlier to offer guests a place to dance.

When I scanned the great room to find Blake, I saw he'd set up a microphone for Scotty, whom I didn't see. The pianist took his break, and Blake moved to the mic. "I hoped to have a guest artist with us today, but he won't be able to join us. In his place, I've been asked by my son-in-law to play a song on the banjo. I hope you'll enjoy it."

During the banjo tune, Tauni waved with her pinky when she scooted by me with a plate of food. She chose a seat next to Wes. Nicki danced, laughed, and clapped. She ran to Blake when he finished and hugged him.

The pianist returned and couples gathered on the dance floor.

Blake took my hand. "Would you like to dance?"

"Do you plan to sing to me too?"

"No, but I may whisper sweet nothings in your ear." His eyes twinkled.

We moved to the center of the room.

I took Blake's hand in mine and placed my other hand on his shoulder. "You impressed me with your banjo playing."

"Nobody else noticed." He chuckled. "Nicki stole

the show."

I glanced around the dance floor and saw Tauni and Wes dancing together too. They looked cute, but they weren't couple material. At least I didn't think so.

The song ended, and we talked with a few guests. While Blake spoke to Walt about a football game, I scanned the gathering of people. Andy and Zoey danced to a romantic song. Easy to tell they were sweet on each other. His gaze and her smile. *They'll make it.*

After Walt sat, I grabbed Blake's arm. "Do you see that?" I jerked my head in the direction of where Tauni and Wes sat.

"What?"

"Wes and Tauni. They're holding hands."

"Maybe another romance in bloom, but what happened to Mitch?"

I shrugged and told him about their breakup. "But Wes is too old for her."

"Let them be. She's a grown woman. He's a good man. I think they'd make a great couple. Age shouldn't have anything to do with it."

"Would you say that if she were Allison?"

"Probably not. But she's not Allison—let her be." He wrapped his arm across my shoulder. "Why are you meddling in other people's affairs when you should be focused on me?"

"Don't you worry. I've thought about you plenty." I winked.

"Would you like anything from the dessert table?" Blake craned his neck to get a view of all the treats.

"Nothing for me."

He meandered around guests and tables on his way to the desserts. A few minutes later he returned with a small piece of turtle cheesecake.

"I should have known that's what you'd find over there." I grabbed the fork from his hand and took a bite. "Yum."

He laughed. "I'll know better next time and bring you your own piece."

I turned again toward Tauni and Wes. A younger man, one I didn't know strode up to their table. He spoke to Tauni and pointed to the dance area. She beamed. When she stood, she glanced over at me and gave me a thumbs up. Wes rubbed the back of his neck and shook his head.

"Who's the young man dancing with Tauni?"

Blake turned in their direction. "That's Quade. A friend of mine."

"Why didn't I meet him?"

"He arrived a few minutes after Tauni, while the two of you were talking near the buffet. I greeted him in the foyer without you." Blake looked back at the couple. "We also chatted at the dessert table. He asked who she was, and I told him that she's available. You know, because Wes is too old for her."

I swatted his arm in a playful gesture. "Are you playing matchmaker?"

He waggled his eyebrows.

"Someone recently told me not to meddle in other people's affairs. So, you don't listen to what you say?"

He offered me his hand. "Another dance?" He set his empty plate on a nearby table and escorted me to the dance floor.

I wrapped both arms around Blake's neck and melted into his embrace. "Well?" I gazed into his eyes and spoke in a light tone. "Should I not pay attention to what you say? Because you don't seem to take your own advice."

He dipped his head and spoke into my ear. "I didn't think you'd mind me talking with Quade about Tauni. With the changes I've seen in her, Quade's a better match than Mitch." He leaned back and guided me past Allison and Jim to avoid a collision. "Without my help, I doubt that they'd meet again before our wedding. I wanted to give them a head start." He narrowed his eyes. "Are you upset with me for interfering?"

"Not at all." I caressed his cheek. "A side of you that surprises me, and I think it's sweet." I bit my lower lip, closed my eyes, and took a calming breath. "Has Andy said anything to you? He didn't act like himself earlier today. Was he nervous regarding the party, or is he upset about us?"

Blake rested his forehead on the top of my head. "He said something this morning. He needs a little time." He lifted my chin and kissed me. "All will be fine." The song ended. "Andy's motioning to me. I'll be right back."

"You're leaving me already?"

"I won't be gone long. He's standing over there." Blake pointed near the dessert table and kissed the top of my head.

A good time for me to check on our guests. I made my way to a table where three of our executives sat. We chatted a few minutes about Blake's excellent chef before I moved on to the next table. There, I thanked my friends from church for celebrating with us. Before I could stop at Chad and Beth's table, I heard a loud giggle through the microphone. "Mommy. I need to ask you something. Where are you?"

Cuteness. I hurried to Nicki and took her by the hand. "Come with Nana. I'll help you find Mommy."

We took two steps. "But I want to ask her if I can tell everyone—."

"Hush, sweetie." I clamped my hand over her mouth.

Not sure if the mic picked up what she said or not, but Carl did. He came to her rescue to help her find Jenny too.

"What does she want to tell everyone?" He cocked his head and squinted at me.

"Why don't you go find Jenny. I'll keep an eye on Nicki." Carl darted toward the kitchen.

I crouched next to Nicki. "I don't know if your mommy told your daddy yet about your baby brother. I think we need to ask her in private."

"I wasn't gonna say anything 'bout *him*. I wanted to tell everyone that I love my new papa."

When I stood, Nicki grabbed my hand, and we moved away from the noisy conversation and laughter. When we stepped into the foyer, Jenny and Carl came down the hallway that led to the kitchen.

Nicki pulled away from me and ran to her mommy. Carl and Jenny were close enough that I could hear them talking. Nicki asked Jenny her question.

Jenny laughed. "Sure. That's fine."

Blake glided toward me.

"Can we talk for a minute? I have great news." He beamed. "My son's coming home."

I reached up and cupped his cheek in my palm. "Will be nice to have them nearby."

After Jenny, Carl, and Nicki strolled toward the great room, Blake said, "What do you think about Andy and Zoey moving into my in-law quarters?"

"Sounds perfect. After we're married, maybe they could live in my condo. More privacy for them."

"Are you wanting them to have privacy or us?" He grinned, and the corner of his eyes crinkled. "I think this will be fun—married to you." He took my hand in his and kissed my fingers.

My heart melted. I led him back to the great room. "Nicki wants to make an announcement to our guests."

Blake peered at Nicki standing at the microphone.

Her face lit when she caught his eye. After she told everyone she loved her new papa, she returned the mic to the lowered stand and ran into Blake's arms.

He held her close and kissed her cheek. After Blake stood, Nicki scampered back to Jenny.

Blake took my hand again. "Your granddaughter is precious."

"Don't you mean, our granddaughter?" I stared into his eyes. "I anticipate sharing her and the rest of my family with you for many years to come."

"And mine with you." He led me toward the kitchen. "I have something for you." We strolled to his refrigerator where he pulled out a salmon colored rose. "I'm excited to no longer need Jim's help to share this expression of my love with you. My dear K, you are my one-and-only."

Movement on the stairway that led from the kitchen to the second floor caught my attention. Andy. He darted back up the steps when he saw me glance his way.

Blake handed me the rose. "And I look forward to our future together." He pulled me closer. "My promise to you. I will love you unconditionally with the love of

God. He's first. Our marriage will be built upon Him. If you don't feel I'm living as the husband you need, leading you as the Lord desires, I want you to set me straight." He kissed me and held me close. "I love you."

I pulled back and placed my hand on his chest. "We better get out there and enjoy our party." I placed the flower inside the refrigerator. "I'll take the rose home with me tonight."

Back in the great room, the pianist played a familiar tune. "Did you ask him to play 'Amazing Grace?'"

Blake placed his arm across my shoulder and led me to the piano, where guests and family gathered.

"A beautiful reminder of my new life and a new year, with my soon-to-be wife." He pulled me closer for another tender kiss.

But my thoughts were on Andy. *He needs a little time—for what? To accept me? I thought he had.* An uneasy feeling settled around my heart. *He won't try to come between Blake and me, will he?*

Twenty-two

At the end of the next song, Nicki ran over to where Blake and I sat in a row of chairs along the back of the great room. She asked Blake to sit with her at a table. There was one seat left, and she wanted to sit in his lap. I told him that I'd be fine, and she'd be thrilled to have him close by. He kissed the top of my head, and they strolled hand in hand. I remembered the picture she'd drawn the week before. *My sweet grandchild.*

Such a blessing to see the two of them together. My granddaughter and her papa to be. They were both beaming at one another while they walked. When Blake sat at the table, Nicki crawled into his lap and laid her head on his chest. Such a special bond the two of them shared—like she and Sam.

I sat back, closed my eyes, and thanked God. A beautiful day and celebration of not only my love and commitment to Blake and his to me but our shared love for the Lord. *Thank you, for blessing me with Blake. Your plans were much better than mine.*

Jenny startled me when she grabbed my arm. "Mom." She spoke close to my ear. "Someone's here to see you." She straightened, her face ashen, and concern edged her voice. "Carl has her in the sitting room. He'll stand guard outside the French doors." She grasped my hand and pulled me up off the chair.

I didn't understand what or who she was referring to. My chest tightened. *Why would Carl need to stand guard?* I peered toward the table where Blake sat with Nicki. They were gone. *Where did he go?*

Jenny pulled me toward the front door. "We'll get her out of here as quickly and secretly as possible."

I stopped, touched the base of my neck, and gaped at Jenny. "Who's here?"

Her chin quivered. "Eliza Walker."

A Note from LuAnn

Dear Reader,

Thank you for reading *Let Him Go*. If you enjoyed Blake and Keedryn's story, please leave a review to help other readers discover it.

I hope you'll join me for *Charm and Perfection*—Book 3 in my *Love Comes Again* series.

Keedryn hopes to get busy making double wedding plans for her and Blake along with Andy and Zoey. But when Andy refuses to move back to Nashville or have a double ceremony, plans fall apart.

Wrapped up in uncertainty with Andy along with deceit and petty crimes, Keedryn and Blake disagree on what actions to take. With the conflict they experience, she wrestles with what her future holds with him and must trust the Lord and not her heart.

Will Keedryn find the strength she needs from God to embark on a lifelong journey with Blake?
Or will she choose the simple life she enjoyed before Blake captured a piece of her heart?

To be notified when future books are released, including *Charm and Perfection*, please sign up for my blog and e-newsletter at www.luannkedwards.com.

Let's connect. I'd love to hear from you!

Website's contact page:
https://www.luannkedwards.com/take-action
Amazon author page:
www.amazon.com/author/luannkedwards
Facebook: https://www.facebook.com/luannkedwards
Twitter: https://twitter.com/LuAnnKEdwards1

Thank you, and God bless!

LuAnn

Acknowledgements

I'm so grateful to my Lord and Savior, and again I thank You for the continuing story of hope you birthed within my heart.

To my husband and family who get excited with me as another book is completed, thank you for your love, support, and encouragement to keep writing.

I'm thankful for my beta readers who shared great ideas and improvements along the way. Thank you, Gerry, Glenda, Helga, Julie, Kim, Kiran, Leah, Moss, and Wendy. I appreciate each one of you for giving your time to this project.

Thank you, Larry J. Leech II for your thorough critique, assistance, and as the story's final pair of eyes before I sent it to the publisher.

Finally, I would like to thank Winged Publications, Forget Me Not Romances for the opportunity to publish my debut series.

Author Bio

LuAnn writes Christian contemporary romance for women who enjoy a wholesome love story that inspires faith and hope. She holds a bachelor's degree from Lee University in Cleveland, Tennessee. LuAnn is a member of American Christian Fiction Writers and has attended several writers' conferences. She grew up in Ohio, lived in Tennessee for many years, and currently resides in New Mexico with her husband of forty-five years. LuAnn adores her children, grandchildren, puggle Pebbles, and cat Paka. A former mathematics teacher and administrative professional, she enjoys reading, hiking, traveling, and spending time with her family. You may find her online at www.luannkedwards.com to learn more about her *Love Comes Again* series.

Sign up for Forget Me Not Romances newsletter and receive a special gift compiled from Forget Me Not Authors!

Join our FB pages to keep up on our most current news!

Forget Me Not Romances Readers and Authors
Take Me Away Books
Winged Publications
Soaring Beyond

www.ingramcontent.com/pod-product-compliance
Lightning Source LLC
Chambersburg PA
CBHW070458200726
48293CB00007B/2280